Brianna R. Shaffery

Dustjacket Art: Saint Jupiter

Cover Art: Ireen Chau

Headshot by Glamour Shots | Photographer: Marko Bulahan | Hair & Makeup: Tatiana Rosa

Published by B.R.S. Writes L.L.C.

Printed in the United States of America

First Printing, 2025

Table of Contents

For my parents, for always supporting me.

Chapter One

Adelaide

Adelaide's eyes roved over the imposing stone castle waiting for her at the end of the drive. A part of her wanted to appreciate the estate's beauty and the peace that radiated from the picturesque courtyard, but Adelaide knew better. A beautiful wrought-iron gate sat wide open at its mouth, welcoming anyone who would dare to step foot inside the fortress masked by tall trees and stone walls.

By the time Adelaide completed her mission, Castle Belmont would not welcome her. In fact, if all went well, the entire province would be vying for the reward her capture would bring them.

After four years, Adelaide should be used to it. But in truth, her heart never ceased to beat with a pang of sadness when each assignment came to an end and she had to return to Mistress Scrabs's clutches. It was a pain she shouldn't know at only twenty-six. In a way, this estate symbolized freedom. Yet it was only another burden for her to shoulder until she'd gotten what Mistress Scrabs had sent her here for.

Until then, Castle Belmont and its vast estate wouldn't—*couldn't*—mean anything to her.

Adelaide swallowed thickly. A shudder threatened to trail down her spine. Aside from rumor and speculation, she knew very little of the fortress that was Castle Belmont. She prayed the steward wouldn't realize her nervousness or see through the forged recommendation Mistress Scrabs had provided her with. If he suspected anything about her was amiss, he'd tell Archduke Hughes, better known as the White Hawk of Kordouva, and he would throw her out of his service before she even stepped foot through the door.

And if he did…Adelaide curled her hands into fists. Archduke Hughes would be the least of her worries if she was found out. Her stomach churned.

Adelaide smoothed down her skirts and straightened her fraying cloak. Gritting her teeth, she took a step up the pathway. The gallop of hooves reached her ears. Turning her head in its direction, Adelaide gasped. Jumping back, her foot slipped, stumbling on a rock.

"Oof," Adelaide groaned, landing on her bottom, her back half buried in the spindly shrubbery that lined the dirt road leading to Castle Belmont's cobblestone driveway. Sitting up, Adelaide raised her hand to brush away the stray strands of her brown hair that had fallen from her braid. Hissing, she glared at her throbbing wrist.

A steady voice called out. The racing horses stopped in their tracks several yards away. Adelaide didn't dare glance their way. Instead, she focused on righting her clothes. The crunch of gravel under booted feet met her ears. Her face burned. She wished she'd left her hair down so she could hide. Before she could even pick herself up and hope it was just happenstance that the men had stopped their horses, a hand appeared in her field of vision.

"Are you all right, miss?" The soft voice coaxed Adelaide into glancing up. It belonged to a man with striking blue eyes and a strong jaw. Stunned by the depths of the man's eyes, Adelaide nearly forgot how to breathe. His jet-black hair was slightly askew from the winter wind, but suited him well. Adelaide blinked hard. Her throat tightened, terrified by the man's undivided attention. Her mind finally made sense of the seconds passing by.

But was this who she thought it was? She dropped her gaze as her mind called forth the sketch of Castle Belmont's master Mistress Scrabs had given her to study. *Archduke Hughes?*

Managing to overcome her paralysis, Adelaide stammered, "Y-yes, thank you, Your Grace."

Foolishly, she accepted his hand. The moment he helped her up, she winced, having already forgotten about her wrist. She bit back her groan.

"Most people who are 'all right' don't wince," Archduke Hughes said, observing her closely. "If you're injured, say so."

"I…well, it's my wrist," Adelaide finally conceded. "But I'm sure it's just a minor sprain. Thank you for your concern, Your Grace."

The Archduke hummed, his lips pursed. He didn't ask as he grasped hold of her hand once more and gingerly maneuvered it to examine her wrist.

"William, don't just stand there. Bring me my bag," he called to the other rider.

Adelaide glanced over at William and watched as he encouraged the massive beasts forward. He was a bit shorter than Archduke Hughes, and fair-haired, though his face was kind and familiar in a way that a friend's should be. They seemed to be the same age, but Adelaide couldn't say for certain, knowing how deceiving looks could be.

Keeping hold of the horses' reins, William managed to free Archduke Hughes's bag and hand it to him. "And to think making sure the horses didn't wander wasn't being helpful enough, Gavin."

Adelaide's mind spun as she realized she was in the presence of not one, but two powerful nobles. Two powerful and *dangerous* nobles, should she be caught. Adelaide squirmed where she stood. The archduke hadn't released her hand and, by the looks of it, had no intention of letting her go anytime soon.

Setting his leather bag down on the dusty gravel by his feet, Archduke Hughes bent slightly and rummaged through it. He pulled a roll of cloth from its confines and straightened. As he began to wrap her wrist, he asked, "What brings you to Castle Belmont?"

Adelaide rubbed her lips together before responding, glancing toward the shadow of the trees so she wouldn't have to look at either of them. "I was hoping to apply for the maid's opening within Your Grace's household."

The archduke paused. Adelaide met his curious gaze and dropped her eyes again, wrapping her free arm around her middle.

"And what recommendations do you have, Miss...perhaps I should ask your name first?" Archduke Hughes asked, as he finished wrapping her wrist.

"Adelaide, Your Grace." Adelaide tried to ignore the burning sensation at the tip of her tongue. Why had she used her real name? What was it about this situation, this man, that made her forget her purpose? "As for my recommendations, I have a letter from Lord Ventner."

"I haven't seen you at his estate. How long were you in his employ?"

Mistress Scrabs's husky voice grated against Adelaide's memory. "For six years, Your Grace."

"And why were you let go?" Archduke Hughes released his hold on Adelaide's hand at last. There wasn't any relief to be had of the action as she blanched at his interrogation. Especially when he left no room for her to recover. "If you were in fact employed by Lord Ventner, I know he doesn't let good help part ways if he can help it, so either you were let go or something else brought you to my estate. So which is it?"

The internal scars Adelaide bore from years of harsh punishments flared sharply as if they'd been freshly inflicted. Despite his brief act of kindness in tending to her injury, Archduke Hughes's reputation as the king's shrewd advisor and unyielding sword wasn't something to be forgotten.

"My mother," Adelaide started cautiously, trying to keep the tremor from her voice. "She's fallen ill, Your Grace, and can no longer take care of herself. I had hoped to be closer to her so that I might care for her."

Adelaide kept her eyes on the ground between them, her head bowed in subservience. The weight of the archduke's eyes on her made Adelaide want to curl in on herself. But she couldn't. She needed to persevere, no matter how uncomfortable the archduke's attention on her made her. This wasn't supposed to be happening. Not once, at any other estate she'd been sent to, had the nobility ever paid her—or any of the servants—any mind.

"Well," he started, "if there is one thing you should know about working in my estate, it's that I do not like people who cannot meet my eyes."

Adelaide's blood froze. Had she heard him right?

"I find them untrustworthy. People who cannot meet the eyes of another are expendable."

"Gavin," William said, his voice full of warning, but Archduke Hughes cut him off.

"Excuse me. I have very important matters to attend to. Sir Maxwell will see you to the estate."

"Thank you, Your Grace," Adelaide managed to say as he turned away and reached for the reins of his speckled horse. Without another word, Archduke Hughes mounted his horse. Adelaide held his bright blue eyes as he glanced back at her and dipped his head before flicking the reins. His horse took off at a trot before breaking into a gallop.

Dust kicked up and clouded the pathway in the aftermath, leaving Adelaide and Sir Maxwell staring after Archduke Hughes through a haze. Adelaide still couldn't wrap her mind around the strange encounter. The White Hawk of Kordouva had stopped to wrap her wrist, but had carried out their conversation with a crisp detachment that directly contradicted the kind action. What sort of man was he really? Was his serious manner a reflection of what was in his heart? Or was there something more to Archduke Gavin Hughes, the king's fiercest ally, than the rumors hinted?

Sir Maxwell cleared his throat. "Should we carry on then, Miss Adelaide?"

Startled from her thoughts, Adelaide snapped her eyes toward the travel-worn knight. "Oh! There's no need to wait for me. I'm sure there are more important things for you to do than escort me to Castle Belmont." Offering him a curtsy, she added, "Thank you for the generous offer, Sir."

"Nonsense," he said. "The walk would do me some good, and I'm sure Viktor wouldn't mind the break from carrying me on his back."

"If it really wouldn't inconvenience you…" Adelaide replied, choosing her words delicately. "I would be grateful for the company."

"Wonderful." Sir Maxwell switched Viktor's reins from one hand to the other and began to step foot down the pathway. Adelaide reached for her bag, but before she could settle its strap on her shoulder, Sir Maxwell said, "Allow me."

"Oh, I can manage, thank you," Adelaide protested.

Sir Maxwell smiled and gripped her bag firmly. "What sort of knight would I be if I let an injured person carry their own bag in my presence?"

"If you insist, Sir." A headache began to pound in Adelaide's temples. How she would ever make it through the interview with Belmont's steward, she hadn't the slightest idea.

"I do insist," Sir Maxwell said, keeping pace with Adelaide as though they had known each other all their lives. "I don't mean to pry, but you said your mother was ill?"

Adelaide's heart stopped. She blinked hard to clear her thoughts. It wasn't exactly a lie; her mother *was* ill. The price of her treatment was what had led Adelaide to fall into Mistress Scrabs's clutches, but how much could she truly reveal about herself before someone found her out?

"Yes." Adelaide pushed the word past her lips. Her tongue turned numb, but still she carried on if only so Sir Maxwell wouldn't be suspicious of her silence. Adelaide did her best to weave a lie she could remember, a lie that blended enough of the truth but still protected her identity—and Mistress Scrabs's ill intentions.

Chapter Two

Gavin

Long shadows stretched across the study. Candlelight flickered over his desk from the plain chandelier overhead. Papers lay before him, unseen and untouched for some time. Sitting with his hands clasped over his midsection, Gavin leaned back in his chair.

Why had that woman come to his estate?

Obviously, the position in his household was a coveted spot, but the opening had hardly been announced in the archduchy's paper, let alone a publication in Caroshire where Lord Ventner's estate was located. Could word truly spread that quickly?

Or had his plan worked so quickly? He'd have to ask for a paper to be brought from Caroshire to be certain.

Staring at the shadows that ebbed and flowed with the clouds, Gavin's mind churned over an endless sea of possibilities. They all hinged on one fact and one fact alone. In all the years Gavin had known Lord Ventner and visited his estate, never once had he seen her. Adelaide. Surely he'd remember someone with such brilliant green eyes. Or who radiated an air of such peace that it stirred his heart and seemed to draw him to her. It was strange how someone like that tried so hard to be invisible, and yet, when he'd told her to, she'd managed to meet his eyes.

She was a most curious woman. Gavin didn't know what to make of her and her appearance at Castle Belmont and, by virtue, his life. All he could do was wait patiently until Thomas came and put an end to his endless conspiracies.

After all, Adelaide hadn't lied about her mother. That he was sure of. Gavin couldn't say if he believed all she'd said, but he did believe someone very close to Adelaide was ill.

Everything else was dependent upon Thomas's report. The best lies bore some truth. It would make it easier to build a persona believable enough to gain entry to some of Kordouva's most powerful houses, his own included. Then there was the timing to consider. Adelaide had appeared much too soon after he'd ordered the advertisement to be printed to have made it all the way from Caroshire.

But if her mother were truly ill, perhaps Adelaide had already left Caroshire and returned home, hoping to find work. Couldn't her appearance be mere coincidence? Would the Master of Thieves really fall prey to an obvious trap such as Castle Belmont hiring a maid when he hadn't hired any staff in close to three years?

Pushing back his chair, Gavin stretched his stiff muscles, shaking out his legs, and took a few stilted steps toward the window. He would be glad if he didn't travel ever again. Or, at least, if he hadn't the need to travel as swiftly or hard ever again.

If it wasn't for their cargo, he and William could have stopped more frequently and taken their time. Aves and Viktor certainly wouldn't have minded the slower pace. He'd have to bring them carrots in the morning to make up for it.

Looking out over his mother's prized gardens, Gavin's eyes gravitated in the direction of the stables beyond them. Maybe he should deliver their gift tonight and try to get back into Aves's good graces as soon as he could. Though the majestic steed hadn't so much as whinnied at their brisk travel, Gavin couldn't help but feel guilt for what the last fortnight had been for him. If his body ached, it was a safe bet to wager that Aves and Viktor would need some time to recover as well before Gavin's cousin, King Jameson Greycove, sent him on another mission to ensure the sovereignty of the kingdom.

Gavin rolled his eyes and crossed his arms. Not all of his cousin's errands were of equal importance, but this one…

This one was unlike any other. He wondered if Jameson understood the power he'd just gifted him, or if he was wholly ignorant of what their bounty was truly capable of—and the threat it could pose if it fell into the wrong hands.

An artifact that could amplify the magic of its user…Gavin pressed his lips together. In the hands of Jameson, it wouldn't have a terrible impact on the world, as there would presumably be more powerful mages than even him. But in the hands of someone like Lady Alyton, the Eye of Behelwer could be catastrophic.

At the mere thought of Lady Alyton, Gavin's mood soured. It wasn't any secret that Lady Alyton sought a power she couldn't herself possess. Control, influence, the hand of the king. She'd even tried to propose marriage to Gavin, no doubt settling for the title of "archduchess" if she couldn't be queen. He feared she'd stop at nothing to wield power over others, and if his suspicions that the infamous Master of Thieves—or "Mistress Scrabs" as she was sometimes known—and Lady Alyton were one and the same, his concern was all the more valid.

Strong raps called Gavin's attention away from the window.

"Enter."

"If His Grace isn't busy," the airy voice of Belmont's steward,

Thomas, drifted over from the doorway, "I should like to make my report."

Gavin regretfully turned his back on the window and gestured for Thomas to join him inside the office.

"What do you make of her?" he asked once the door was firmly shut against prying ears.

"Adelaide seems quiet, but not timid. I believe she has great potential, even in spite of her wrist," Thomas started, staring at him pointedly. Gavin sighed and meant to offer an excuse but found he hadn't the time. "She believes she will be fine by tomorrow, though I am no physician. Until her wrist is healed, she will be given lighter duties. I do have one concern though, Your Grace."

Gavin's lips twisted into a frown. "Which is?"

Thomas pulled a folded letter from the inner pocket of his waistcoat. "I believe her letter of recommendation was forged."

"What makes you think so?" Gavin asked. He accepted the offered letter and glanced over it. Upon first inspection, it seemed like Lord Ventner's writing to him. Squinting, he studied it with a harsh eye.

"If you look at the spacing of the first few lines, you'll notice slight flooding of the letters, meaning someone hesitated or was taking their time with their crafting of the letter. This does not appear in the later paragraphs, as the letters are noticeably lighter and thinner as they became more confident in their writing." Gavin nodded, knowing well enough that Thomas, the man who'd had a hand in helping to raise him, wasn't quite finished. "And I happen to know on good authority that Lord Ventner, like his father, uses a particular ink. This is not it. It's much too thin, cheap."

Gavin tossed the letter carelessly down on his desk. His lips quirked into a small smile. "Would that authority be you, Thomas?"

"It would be, Your Grace." Thomas returned his smile, straightening just a bit as though pleased Gavin had remembered his previous tenure as the late Lord Ventner's steward. But the smile faded away, and with it the humor of the previous moment. "How would you like to proceed regarding Adelaide, Your Grace? I know you had asked that the position be hers, but given this development, it seems counterintuitive to allow her near-limitless access to the estate."

Gavin clasped his hands behind his back. Studying the carpet, he began to pace. His mind spun, returning to his earlier theories and adding to the heap of potential accusations that had accumulated in his mind. Even more than that, his curiosity nagged at him. Coming to a halt, Gavin closed his eyes and took a breath before facing Thomas once more. He thought of the advertisement and his hopes that Mistress

Scrabs would answer it once more. "Keep an eye on her. We'll proceed carefully until we know more about her and what her intentions are. I want to be certain of who she is before we take any action."

"As you wish, Your Grace." Thomas bowed his head. "Is there anything else I can do for you before taking my leave?"

"No." Gavin shook his head, plopping back down in his desk chair. "Thank you and goodnight, Thomas."

"Goodnight, Your Grace."

As the door clicked shut behind the steward, Gavin let out a heavy sigh.

Whatever Adelaide had come here for, he was certain it was for no good cause. His gaze dropped to the letter on his desk. Taking hold of it, Gavin skimmed over it once more, trying to pick out anything that could direct him in discovering Adelaide's motive. But after several long minutes of examining it and holding it up to the candlelight, nothing revealed itself to him. So instead, he resigned to add it to the mounting pile of papers related to his investigation.

"*Coopenell,*" Gavin murmured. With a click, the hidden drawer of his desk slid open, and Gavin dropped the letter inside the folder that held letters from his informant, witness testimonies, and the grievances of the burglarized. Shutting it, he stood and stretched his legs, assured by the audible slide of the magical lock replacing itself.

Tomorrow, he would resume his investigation anew. That, and ensure the Eye of Behelwer didn't wreak havoc within his province.

Chapter Three

Adelaide

Adelaide snuggled deeper into the warmth surrounding her, not yet wanting to wake from the dream of a soft bed and a satisfied stomach. She just knew that if she opened her eyes, she would find herself either in some dingy inn lying on a bed stuffed with straw or worse. She'd always rather be at an inn than the room Mistress Scrabs had assigned to her at the auction house.

"Miss Adelaide?" a calm voice called, though muffled. "It's time to get up, or you'll miss your chance for breakfast before your duties!"

Adelaide forced herself to sit up, blinking away the remainder of her sleep. "Breakfast?" she muttered. Her heart stopped. Full awareness slammed into her and nearly knocked her out of the comfortable bed. When she glanced across the room, the bed where the other maid had slept was already made up and no doubt cold. Swearing under her breath, Adelaide scrambled out of bed. Mindful of her tender wrist, Adelaide hastily changed and pulled her hair back.

Wrenching the door open, Adelaide stopped short. Cathy smiled back at her, seemingly unaware that Adelaide had nearly knocked into her in her haste.

"Sorry, I didn't mean to make you think you had to rush. I just didn't want you to miss breakfast, and since you came from such a long way," the brunette rambled, "we thought it was best to let you sleep a while longer than the rest of us."

"Besides," another started as she passed by, a thick accent in her voice, "you missed the stable hand's attempt at serenading us while Ned fixed breakfast."

Cathy giggled. "I thought it was entertaining."

The maid with the accent—Juliana, Adelaide remembered—rolled her eyes. "That's because you fancy Jacob."

Adelaide found herself smiling, watching as Cathy looped her arm through Juliana's and carried on in their journey down the narrow hall. The pair hardly fit down the aisle side by side.

Glancing back at her, Cathy asked, "Are you coming, Addie?"

Adelaide blinked at the nickname, her face warming. "Yes."

"Don't worry. You'll get used to things here in no time. You might even like it here in spite of the circumstances that brought you to us!" Cathy smiled.

Adelaide was still staring after them in wonder as the hall opened up into the galley kitchen where Ned was cleaning up their breakfast things. A place setting had been set aside for Adelaide.

"Eat your fill, love," he said. "You've got a long day ahead of you."

Adelaide thanked him, uncertain if that was a warning or a simple fact. Either way, she wasn't about to let the colorful plate of food go to waste.

Maybe…maybe she could take her time in acquiring the Eye of Behelwer for Mistress Scrabs.

Chewing slowly, Adelaide wondered how long she could dawdle before the Master of Thieves sent someone after her. Suppressing a shudder, the rational part of her mind asked if she was willing to find out the cost of such a slight against Mistress Scrabs.

Adelaide's nose tingled. There had to be tens of thousands of portraits and vases and odd artifacts that needed dusting throughout the estate. She didn't think her heart could withstand another sneeze, and she still had the entire third floor of the castle to dust.

In the time she'd spent dusting the first floor of Castle Belmont, she'd noted that few guards were stationed throughout the mansion. She only saw them at the entrances and exits, and hadn't seen one since coming up to the second floor. It struck her as odd, though a part of her was relieved. Maybe that would make finding what she was looking for easier, and she'd be able to do so quickly.

But would the White Hawk of Kordouva really be so foolish as to leave his estate unguarded? Surely he wasn't. Adelaide tilted her head, staring at the portrait she'd just finished dusting. She didn't know who it was, though she wouldn't doubt it was yet another Hughes ancestor. They were all starting to look the same to her. Blue eyes, stern expression, rich clothing. It was uncanny. For all she knew, she was staring at a portrait of the archduke himself. Though she supposed the trim beard gave away the fact that this was not the current head of Castle Belmont.

Adelaide's mind returned to the problem at hand. If there were no guards, then how did Archduke Hughes protect his estate and all the valuables hidden within? Would she even be able to find, access, and steal what she'd come here for?

Or would she end up dead by some tragic mistake, struck down by a power she didn't anticipate?

Surely that was more likely. His reputation didn't lead her to believe that the castle was as open as it appeared. For someone the rumors painted as hardened by battle and more perceptive than his relatively young age should allow, could Castle Belmont truly be undefended? There *had* to be something guarding every nook and cranny of the grand estate.

"Hello, Miss Adelaide." Archduke Hughes's voice broke through her thoughts, making her flinch. "I'm sorry. I didn't mean to startle you, though if I'm honest, I didn't expect to find anyone up here."

"Hello, Your Grace." Adelaide bobbed a curtsy and offered a polite smile, still uncertain about meeting his eyes. The authority the archduke had wielded yesterday when he'd warned her about the importance of eye contact in his estate still made her uneasy.

How could she look them all in the eye and know she was lying to them every single day? She wouldn't survive if she did.

"How is your wrist?" he asked, gesturing to the wrapping she still wore.

"It's better," Adelaide responded, forcing herself to lift her head and at least stare at his face. She hoped it would be enough to satisfy the archduke's rule. "Though still a little tender. Thank you for asking, Your Grace."

"I'm sure it will be much better in a few days," he said, almost convincing Adelaide it would. "So aside from dusting, what else have you been tasked with?"

Adelaide nearly frowned. Why would the archduke care about her and her duties? In all the estates she'd infiltrated, never once had anyone, least of all the master of the estate, ever taken any interest in her. "Just the dusting for now, though I'll be helping with the laundry beginning tomorrow as well."

"At least the laundry room is warm. Training in the grounds this time of year is difficult."

Adelaide couldn't say she was used to the province's winters, not if she intended to keep the ruse that she'd come from Lord Ventner's estate in the north of Kordouva. She forced herself to smile. "Very true, Your Grace."

Clearing his throat, Archduke Hughes stepped away. "I suppose I should go about my own duties and leave you to yours."

"Thank you, Your Grace." Adelaide didn't like how quiet her voice had gone.

This was always the hardest part of any assignment Mistress Scrabs sent her on. She hated it, trying to figure out the dynamic of the estate and the people within its walls. Every time, Adelaide was forced to assess who was safe, who posed a threat to her, and who might realize why she'd come. And no matter how friendly people were toward her,

Adelaide couldn't allow them to seep into her life, regardless of whether or not she enjoyed their company or wanted to know them better.

She didn't know how many more times she could steal for Mistress Scrabs before word began to spread of a maid with brown hair and green eyes who had a penchant for stealing. How it hadn't already was almost insulting. Did the people she stole from truly not make the connection between her appearance at their estate and subsequent disappearance, along with one of their valuables?

Surely by now someone would have made the connection—unless she was truly as forgettable as Mistress Scrabs harshly praised her for.

Adelaide slumped and sent a longing gaze toward the portrait. But the painted face of the Hughes ancestor offered her no words of encouragement or contradiction to the Master of Thieves's faux compliment.

Chapter Four

Gavin

Remind me again of the report given by Lady Estelle Marlon?" Gavin paced in front of the large bay window in his office. He hoped talking through his suspicions without expressly naming them would prove helpful, that someone aside from himself would come to the same conclusion. But if William didn't, he would have to consider whether or not he was grasping at evidence that was only mere coincidence.

William sighed, "Why are you going back through the reports?"

"I'm testing a theory and hoping to dispel some doubts about our plan to hire a maid." Gavin stopped and glanced out the window. Sunshine filtered through the scattered clouds.

"According to Lady Estelle's complaint, the Mystic's Broach went missing along with the maid she suspected of stealing it."

"Did she give a description of the maid in question?"

Gavin listened to the shuffle of pages as William presumably flipped through them in search of a description. “There doesn’t seem to be one, from anyone. Lady Estelle was only able to say that the maid was frail-like, which I find hard to believe is an accurate description given the nature of being a criminal. The other servants all said she was only there for a few months, and hardly interacted with them. I remember their embarrassment when asked to provide a description of her and they couldn’t. One said she had long hair. Another said she thought it was shoulder length. Some said she was short; others said she was tall. It all contradicts each other.”

“I see. What about Duke Quimbley?”

“What about him?”

“Are there any descriptions of the maid that overlap between reports? Surely between all of them there is something in common.”

“How long have you been studying these, Your Grace?”

Gavin tensed. William only ever called him “Your Grace” when he disapproved of something. Turning to face his friend, Gavin lied, “I’ve only just begun.”

William narrowed his eyes. Clicking his tongue, he set the papers down on the coffee table. “I’m sure.”

Gavin clasped his hands behind his back and turned on his heel. “You don’t find it odd that all of these reports seem to point to a singular woman appearing at these estates and businesses and then disappearing along with or shortly after the item goes missing?"

William sighed, placing Lady Marlon's folder beside the others spread out on the coffee table. "You also tried to convince me that Lady Alyton and Mistress Scrabs were one and the same."

"It's the truth," Gavin said through clenched teeth. "I just have to find irrefutable evidence linking her to the Den of Thieves."

William rolled his eyes. "You need to accept the fact that we aren't any closer than we were six months ago to finding the culprit, and swallow your pride. We need more time. Surely your cousin understands that."

He would, but Gavin couldn't admit that there was something on this earth capable of eluding him.

William crossed his arms. "I can't believe you! You aren't going to admit that you can't—"

"William, enough." Gavin let his arms fall freely to his side. "When the time comes, I will own up to my failings, but as of right now, I have no intention of giving up on this. There *has* to be some connection we're missing."

Leaning back on the sofa, William ran a hand through his hair. "What have you discovered, Gavin? Why the sudden mania?"

Gavin nodded. "I think you'll find some plausibility in my theory."

William snorted. Waving his hand in a show for Gavin to continue, William smiled as if jesting. "I'm sure I will."

Gavin took his cue, explaining the common descriptions—the dark hair, the green or gray eyes, and the fact that the thief was easily overlooked, inconspicuous—that appeared in each report that led him to believe some truth was lying bare before them in the witness testimony. He admitted that while the maid's descriptions were vague and could fit nearly anyone, if they could find some evidence as to how she managed to steal from some of the most prominent homes in Kordouva, they would find their thief. And once they found their thief, they would find Mistress Scrabs.

"I think we're close," Gavin concluded. "Within a few months, we may be able to put an end to the Den of Thieves."

William shook his head. "I don't understand it, but I think I actually agree with you. Everything in the reports matches the descriptions given by our informants, and now that we have a better timeline established rather than that poor excuse for a debrief by the Commander of the Royal Legion, you might be right. This could all end soon. And if I had to guess, I'd say that the Master of Thieves feels confident that enough time has passed since their last theft and is looking to—"

Gavin glared at the door. Who could be knocking during a time in which he explicitly asked not to be disturbed?

"I hope that's lunch." William stood and started for the door. "I'm starving."

Gavin went about organizing the case files and making sure nothing of importance was in plain sight. As William cracked the door open and greeted the person on the other side, Gavin stilled.

"Hello, Miss Adelaide." His friend's voice was steady and without a trace of suspicion. But Gavin's mind harbored plenty for the both of them. How could William act so casually, as if they hadn't spent all morning rereading the witness testimonies and case debriefs for nearly sixty high-profile thefts, all of which pointed to the culprit being a member—a *new* member—of the house's staff?

"Ned has prepared lunch for both you and His Grace." By comparison, Adelaide's voice was hollow and demure. It grated on Gavin. Castle Belmont was safe, no matter who you were. Was she merely intimidated by people with titles? Or, if Gavin's suspicions about the thief were correct and she did infiltrate the services of noble houses, was it an act she put on so as to pass unnoticed?

Gavin shook his head. What was he thinking? Yes, he knew Adelaide was lying about something, but she didn't strike him as someone so conniving. There hadn't been a trace of malice or deception in her eyes. Besides, Adelaide didn't seem like the sort of person people could forget as easily as the thief was. At least, Gavin realized, she'd been on his mind quite a lot since she'd arrived, as he'd grappled between the success of his trap and what might be a twist of fate's humorous timing.

"Thank you, Adelaide," William said, accepting the offered tray and shutting the door behind him once more. Gavin couldn't even hear Adelaide's footsteps walking away from the office. There wasn't even a single *squeak* or protest from the old creaky floors.

It was like she was a ghost.

"What's that look for?" William asked. "Are you upset that Ned was thoughtful enough to send up lunch for us? Or have you discovered something so unpleasant as to glare at thin air?"

Gavin fixed his stare on William, unamused by his loose tongue. "I think you take the bonds of our friendship too liberally, William."

"If it wasn't for me, you wouldn't talk to anyone," he said around bites of the steak Ned had prepared for them.

He couldn't admit that William was right. So instead, he pointedly unfolded his napkin and picked up his utensils. "How's Evelynn? Is she any better?"

William stilled. "She's…not any better. Worse actually. It seems her illness is more serious than I thought when we'd left."

"I'm sorry," Gavin said. "If there's anything I can do to help—"

"Thank you," William said and shook his head. "But I'm sure she'll be fine now that I'm home and can heal her. It may just take a little more effort than I'd thought."

Gavin nodded. "Well, still, let me know. I can handle things with the investigation if you'd rather be by Evelynn's side for the time being."

William hummed. "I'll consider it."

As a stretch of silence overcame them, Gavin retreated into his thoughts. At least now he could rest assured that his theory about the thief had been validated by their conversation this morning.

Now, he only had to catch a thief. Then, he could topple the Den of Thieves once and for all, destroying the foundation of Mistress Scrabs's power.

Gavin donned his cloak and moved stealthily through the castle. He hoped no one would discover him and delay his visit to the stables—or worse, offer to see to Aves themselves so that he might retire for the night or continue his duties as head of the Belmont estate.

Luckily, not a soul had stopped him or crossed his path. From down the hall, he could hear laughter and the chatter of the servants. A small smile tugged at his lips.

Perhaps all his hardships were worthwhile if it could guarantee the happiness and wellbeing of even a small group such as Castle Belmont's staff. In his heart, Gavin knew he'd managed more than that. Every single person who'd stood beside Jameson, himself, and William during the Battle of Rivenfield had made the future—had made *this* moment—possible in spite of Penumbra's shadow.

Contented for a moment, Gavin selected the finest carrots he could find from the bin of root vegetables and set off for the stables.

He turned his collar up against the brisk wind. Lanterns lit the way to the barn. Their glow illuminated the tree-lined path, mingling with the dusky sunlight and presenting Gavin with a calming picture despite the chill in the air. He was glad when he reached the barn and pulled the door shut behind him.

Rubbing his hands together for warmth, Gavin's eyes adjusted to the darkness. The horses snorted and huffed. A few whinnied or stomped their hooves.

"It's only me," he said into the shadows of the barn. The scent of hay tickled his nose. Blowing a warm breath on his hands, Gavin gathered his magic and let it unfurl around him, bringing light to the barn at last.

A loose bunch of hay sat in the feeding tray attached to each stall door. Passing each stall, Gavin was careful to keep the carrots concealed. As he passed by Viktor's stall, the gray steed tried to nip at his cloak. Gavin held a finger up to his lips and hushed him. Gavin offered him a carrot, knowing Viktor had worked just as tirelessly on their journey to transport the Eye of Behelwer. The horse accepted it graciously, making Gavin shake his head. He would be so lucky if Aves greeted him the same way. Moving on to the next stall, Gavin watched as Aves turned his back to the stall door as Gavin stopped to unlatch the bolt.

"I know," he whispered, cautiously stepping inside. Aves's ears twitched. His tail flicked, but the horse's stubborn nature was the only real greeting he offered. "It was a long, hard, and unfair journey, and I'm sorry."

Aves shook his head. His mane rippled with the movement.

Gavin sighed. At least there was some semblance of comfort in the routine.

"I guess I brought these carrots for nothing. You're clearly happy with the hay." Gavin pulled the carrots from beneath his cloak. Aves slowly turned to look at him. Skepticism shone in his dark eyes. Gavin dangled the carrots from his hand. "Oh? Does this mean I'm forgiven?"

Aves stamped his hooves. The noise he made sounded like a grumble. Gavin couldn't help but laugh as Aves maneuvered around and made a quick grab for the carrots. Gavin patted Aves's shoulder as he ate.

"I truly am sorry. I wish we could've had an easier journey, but the—"

Both Gavin and his horse froze as the barn door creaked open. Arching his brow, Gavin reluctantly stepped out of the stall to see who had come and what business likely needed his attention now.

"Your Grace!" Adelaide gushed. "I'm so sorry. I-I didn't realize—"

Gavin held up a hand to stop her. "It's all right."

The pair stood in awkward silence for a moment. Gavin glanced back toward Aves, but the horse didn't offer any advice. Gavin reached a hand up and rubbed the back of his neck, then straightened in an attempt to play the nervous gesture off as though he were merely soothing some ache in his neck.

"What brings you to the stables at this time of night, Miss Adelaide?" It was a fair question, one he knew could easily be asked of him as well. At least he had a viable answer. What could Adelaide be doing in the stables? Was she spying for the Master of Thieves? Or was it something more innocuous?

"I saw the light," she said softly. Gavin studied her closely, from the slope of her shoulders and the slight curl in the tips of her hair to the way her gaze avoided his. Gavin wondered what would happen if their eyes did meet again. Would they strike him as much as they had the first time?

Adelaide's voice seemed to lull him into a sense of peace, even as her words themselves filled him with panic. "I thought perhaps someone was hiding in the barn or…well, I don't know. I just thought it best to investigate and find out, Your Grace."

"Miss Adelaide," he said firmly, hoping to command her attention. Slowly, she dragged her gaze toward him. Gavin swallowed, grateful for the distance between them. Still, he saw the way she wrapped an arm around herself and seemed to shrink at the tone of his voice. His eyes briefly took in the bandage on her opposite wrist. A twist of guilt stabbed him in the gut. A whispered reminder from the back of his mind squashed the guilt as quickly as it had come. He'd placed the advertisement for a maid as a trap. He'd wanted to draw the thief to Castle Belmont, and Adelaide had come as a result of his hopeless effort.

If she truly was the thief, she was playing her part well. But the fact remained that Gavin couldn't prove that she was who he suspected her to be. So instead, he took a breath and tried not to sound so harsh. "If you ever feel there is something amiss, please tell the guards and let them investigate. You need not put yourself in harm's way."

"Yes, Your Grace." Gavin's gut twisted as she offered him a curtsy. "I'll leave you to your night."

Gavin clenched his jaw. He wanted to stop her, to call out and ask her to stay. Instead, he watched her leave without saying another word. Even if he had said something, was there anything that would've made any sense?

Shaking the conflicted mix of curiosity and suspicion from his mind, Gavin returned to Aves. He picked up the brush hung beside the stall door and stroked Aves's muzzle. Slowly, Gavin brushed Aves down in silence. He knew the stable master and hands would've already cared for Aves, but Gavin needed something to keep busy as his mind turned over everything he knew about the Den of Thieves, Mistress Scrabs, and the string of thefts. Somewhere in that jumble of thoughts, Gavin found himself thinking of Adelaide, the enchanting nature of her green eyes, and wondering just how or if she was connected to any of it.

Chapter Five

Adelaide

It was impossible for dust to collect overnight, and yet Adelaide was proven wrong daily. She didn't understand where it all came from, only that it had been her duty to dust the east wing of the castle every single day for the last week and a half.

And in all that time, she'd yet to uncover a single safe or hidden room. Everything was exactly as it should be in Castle Belmont. She began to wonder if the archduke even possessed the Eye of Behelwer. Adelaide wholeheartedly believed if he did, she would have found something by now to indicate its whereabouts in the manor. Or perhaps some rumor whispered amongst the staff.

Adelaide smiled. As she trailed the feather duster over a pristine vase, the memory of their first meeting lingered in the forefront of her mind. Archduke Gavin Hughes was nothing like she expected, and neither was his estate. Of all the places she'd been sent to during her time as Mistress Scrabs's agent, Castle Belmont was by far Adelaide's favorite.

All of the others had had an oppressive air, and mistrust loomed in every corner. Certainly, there'd been a few others she'd liked, but nothing compared to this estate. It was like they were a family. Adelaide had yet to witness conspiratorial whispers between the other maids or find herself the object of guarded scrutiny.

Humming quietly to herself, Adelaide moved along. Studying the empty third floor yet again, the forgotten portraits and gifts and precious family heirlooms offered none of their secrets. There wasn't anything about this wing and this floor that Adelaide hadn't already discovered. Nothing was ever out of place. From day to day, everything was as it had been previously. Adelaide didn't know whether to be disappointed or relieved.

All it meant was that she'd have to stay longer.

But it also meant that the longer she had to stay at the estate, the more likely it was that she would be discovered—or worse, Mistress Scrabs's patience would expire.

Adelaide's heart clenched. Her mind went silent.

She needed to find the archduke's vault, and quickly.

"I didn't mean to disturb you."

Adelaide flinched. The feather duster slipped from her loose hold as the archduke himself stepped into the hallway and paused some feet away from her.

"I hope you don't mind me saying," Archduke Hughes continued as he toed the carpet with the tip of his shoe. Oddly, Adelaide found she couldn't catch his gaze. "You have a lovely voice."

Adelaide opened and closed her mouth. She had only been humming—hadn't she? Adelaide replayed the last few minutes over in her head in a vain attempt to figure out if she really had been singing aloud. "Thank you, Your Grace."

She shifted on her feet. He didn't reply, instead taking a keen interest in the floor. Adelaide spared a glance at the feather duster.

"How is your wrist? Better?" As Adelaide tore her gaze from the fallen duster, she was met by the full weight of the archduke's attention. Her breath hitched, caught by the intricacies hidden in his blue eyes.

"Much better, thank you." She clasped her hands together, fighting the urge to glance away again.

The archduke hummed, though remained silent. Adelaide couldn't tell if she was mesmerized or hallucinating. Was she openly staring at the archduke? Was *he* openly staring at *her*? Adelaide's heart quivered in her throat. The archduke couldn't possibly *see* her, not really. Her singing had likely interrupted his thoughts for only a moment.

Her cheeks heated. Even if it had been nice to believe that, even for a second, Archduke Hughes had experienced the same breathlessness she had, he couldn't possibly be staring at her. He had no reason to, unless he was suspicious of her. Adelaide's chest hollowed.

"Well." Archduke Hughes cleared his throat as he glanced away. "I suppose I should be on my way then…and leave you to the, uh, dusting."

"Oh." Disappointment sank to the pit of her stomach. She shouldn't let herself wish they'd had a moment longer. "Yes, thank you, Your Grace."

The archduke's shoulder accidentally brushed hers as he glided past. Adelaide's heart pounded between her ears. Her mind spiraled as the archduke muttered an apology and nearly tripped over his own feet in an effort to put a respectable distance between them. She couldn't even reply as her throat had gone dry. All she could do was watch him leave as her chest seemed to burn.

What had just happened?

Adelaide counted backwards from ten to compose herself. With her breath regained, she retrieved the duster from the floor and returned to her duties. From the corner of her eye, Adelaide realized the archduke had disappeared around the corner, leaving her alone once more.

Her mind sparked.

Why would the archduke make frequent trips to the all-but-abandoned third floor?

Could it be?

As quietly as she could, Adelaide darted to the end of the hall. Peering around the corner, she observed as Archduke Hughes neared the end of the next hall. Her brows furrowed. What could have brought him? Surely it wasn't a hallway that led nowhere. The archduke raised a hand.

Adelaide's jaw dropped.

The far wall rippled, and the archduke walked right through it.

Chapter Six

Gavin

...and come find me, my love

For the doves have gone

Soarin' through the dawn

Gavin paused, tilting his head. The soft voice carried down the hall, and with it the solemn melody that had swept across Kordouva. He hadn't heard that song since the war had ended. But who could be singing it now? Had he finally lost his mind, succumbed to guilt for all he'd done during the war?

Oh my darling love

I have lost my heart

With hope's depart...

As he drew closer on silent feet, the voice washed away all meaning behind the words. He found himself nearly hypnotized by the layered quality of the voice, like a siren's call. He stopped and let his eyes fall shut. Somehow, this voice, this singer, had turned a mournful melody into one of longing. He found himself almost believing the two lovers in the song would find each other again, and that they would share in peace and life everlasting. His own heart yearned for nothing more, and by the sound of the soothing tone that enveloped him, Gavin knew without a doubt that the singer shared in his dream.

Gavin shifted on his feet. The floorboard betrayed him, groaning loudly in the otherwise quiet hall. The singing stopped.

Gavin cursed himself. He straightened his shoulders and smoothed the front of his shirt down. Fixing a bored expression on his face, he meant to appear as if he hadn't heard the singing in the slightest, and that he most definitely hadn't stopped to listen.

The detachment he tried to instill in his veins shattered the instant he rounded the corner.

Waiting for him there was the very woman he couldn't help but suspect of some deception, and yet, he began to realize, the very same woman his mind often strayed toward for no discernable reason.

"I didn't mean to disturb you," he said quickly.

At the sound of his voice, Adelaide jumped. The duster fell from her hand, and she whirled on him, her green eyes alight with panic.

Guilt clawed at him. Had she truly not heard the floorboard creak?

Gavin studied the carpet. He couldn't stop the words that tumbled from his lips next. "I hope you don't mind me saying you have a lovely voice."

And she did. A voice as gentle and soft, yet sure as Adelaide's demeanor. It made Gavin think of the not-so-far-gone past and the impending eclipse, though he supposed that was more her choice of song than her singing. "Kordouva's Lament" was a song everyone seemed to know. He wondered if that perhaps wasn't the case anymore. Penumbra and Darshovi had been defeated. The generation born in the years since the end of the war would not know the perils theirs and their forebears had.

Perhaps he was wrong. Maybe there were more Kordouvians anxious about the upcoming eclipse than within the walls of Castle Belmont. It was the first eclipse since the end of the war. It would only be natural that his countrymen shared the same concern, the one that had led Gavin to spend months preparing for something that might not come to pass.

"Thank you, Your Grace," she replied quietly. Gavin was almost afraid to look at her. Had he embarrassed her? Made things more awkward than they should have been?

He hoped that wasn't the case. He hadn't meant to witness what he was slowly realizing was a private moment of vulnerability.

Gavin wished he hadn't moved a muscle. He should've just stood there and waited for Adelaide to move along down the hall.

Though there was no guarantee that she hadn't started at the far end and that she would come upon him standing there.

That would have been awkward.

Gavin shook his head slightly to clear the thoughts from his head. His mind grappled for something to say, to fill the silence. Gavin chanced a look at Adelaide. His shoulders dropped in relief. She wasn't even looking at him. Instead, her fixation was on the fallen feather duster. Gavin studied her, the way her hair draped over her shoulders and how it curled softly at the edges and the way the light bounced off her rich brown locks. A spark flitted through his mind. An unassuming maid who appeared at estates and disappeared along with a valuable magical artifact. Could she really be Adelaide?

The realization reminded him of his need to focus, especially if his growing suspicions proved accurate.

Slowly, their eyes met. Once again, Gavin found himself captivated by the glimmer hidden behind the emotions that flitted across her emerald eyes. The dread simmering in his gut and the sense of responsibility tightening in his chest loosened.

To be a good thief was to have power over someone. A good thief went unnoticed. They disarmed people with a charming personality or were so quiet their presence left no trace of a disturbance.

Adelaide drew too much attention to be a thief. Gavin kept wondering if maybe her appearance at the estate was a mistake, a coincidence.

Perhaps the advertisement was too conspicuous. Gavin probably would have had better luck of trapping Mistress Scrabs's thief had he let rumors about him possessing the Eye of Behelwer leak from Castle Belmont.

He'd never been more uncertain about anything as he stared back at Adelaide. He truly didn't know what to make of her as his mind fractured and waged war with itself.

So he said the only thing he could think of. "How is your wrist?"

Adelaide shifted. "Much better, thank you."

Gavin bobbed his head. That was good at least. Even with his latest conspiracy in mind, Gavin wished he knew what to do to assure her that no harm would come to her here at the estate, that she was safe. He also wished he hadn't given himself away, bitter that he'd ruined the chance to hear more of Adelaide's singing.

It was odd how quickly his own vulnerabilities responded to her, regardless of whether or not she was consciously playing them. For that, Gavin couldn't say. He didn't wholly understand what was happening every time their eyes met or when he happened upon her. All he knew was that his chest felt loose, and, for the first time in days, his mind stopped. Adelaide was like the eye of the storm: utterly calm despite the chaos and danger around it.

He didn't know which disturbed him more. The effect that she had on him, or the fact that he didn't mind it.

If only there wasn't that suspicion and the fact that the Master of Thieves would eventually target the Eye of Behelwer.

Clearing his throat, Gavin dragged his eyes away and weakly excused himself. After all, he'd come up here for a reason. As much as he wanted to dawdle, to learn more about Adelaide to satisfy his suspicions, the Eye of Behelwer took precedence. If he didn't stabilize it on a daily basis, there was no way of knowing how destructive its energy would become.

"Well, I suppose I should be on my way then…and leave you to the, uh, dusting."

"Oh." Adelaide's voice dipped. Gavin studied her, noticing the slight downturn of her lips. Had he upset her? Before he could ask, Adelaide gave him a slight curtsy and said, "Yes, thank you, Your Grace."

The dismissal struck his heart. He cursed his tongue, forcing himself to continue on his way. Lost in his own thoughts, Gavin nearly jumped as his shoulder grazed Adelaide's. An apology fell from his lips without hesitation. He hadn't even realized how close he was to her as he'd gone by.

Luckily, Adelaide didn't say a word about the accident. Gavin let out a silent sigh of relief, quickening his footsteps so as not to linger any longer lest he embarrass himself further. Squaring his shoulders, Gavin weakly attempted to shove aside all thoughts of Adelaide, the Master of Thieves, and his investigation. He needed complete and absolute focus for this task. If he wasn't careful, the Eye of Behelwer would consume him, putting everyone at Castle Belmont and possibly the entire province at risk.

Taking a deep breath, Gavin fixed his gaze on the wall at the end of the hallway with its faded paisley wallpaper and chipped wainscotting. He raised his hand. Power emanated from his palm, a gentle fizzle beneath his skin.

The essence of his magic met with the protective wards. Gavin pressed his lips together as the static of the magical barrier rippled through him before it settled, flooding him with a cool sensation. He held his breath as he passed through the wall. His ears popped.

"I hate that," he muttered, shaking his head. Opening and closing his mouth a few times, Gavin let his eyes adjust to the dimness of the vault. The only light came from the few luminous artifacts he'd acquired over the years.

Gavin brought his hands together and slowly pulled them apart. A ball of light formed between the dome of his fingers. Carefully, he pulled wisps of light from the sphere and sent them to the sconces spaced evenly around the room. The wicks of the candles caught flame and sent bouncing light around the cramped vault.

In the very center of all his relics was the crown jewel of them all. The Eye of Behelwer.

A rough vermilion gemstone, the Eye of Behelwer was the only surviving sunstone with its ability.

It was also one of the few magic enhancers Penumbra hadn't destroyed, making the Eye of Behelwer a sought-after artifact.

Prized, but also dangerous. If someone like Mistress Scrabs were to get hold of the Eye, Gavin wasn't certain anyone would be able to stop her, not even him. And if there was any merit to his deepest fears…Gavin pressed his lips in a grim line.

There was only a month until the next solar eclipse, the first since Penumbra's War had ended. But the Eye of Behelwer was in his possession, safe and sound. There was no cause for worry.

Nodding to himself, Gavin held fast to the appeasement offered by his own mind.

He needed to act quickly. The sooner he expelled the stone's buildup of energy, the better. He couldn't spend all day staring at it and theorizing how his unseen—and possibly imagined—enemies might use its natural properties against Kordouva.

Slowly approaching the sunstone, Gavin steeled himself against the waves of nausea that consumed him. Every day, it seemed as though the stone grew stronger, needier. He feared he'd have to increase his visits to twice a day as it fed on the energies of the surrounding artifacts. Closing only half the distance between the hidden entrance and where he'd placed the Eye of Behelwer in the center of the vault, Gavin's knees began to quake. He worried that today would be the day he couldn't even handle the stone. Still, he pushed himself to keep his bearings. Panting, Gavin put one foot in front of the other. Sweat beaded between his brows. Just one more step, that was all.

Gavin couldn't even revel in the relief of coming face to face with the sunstone. He still had to take it in his hands and cast something, anything that wouldn't tear apart the fabric of their world.

Taking the cool stone in his hand, Gavin gritted his teeth and shut his eyes. He would *not* give into the stone's temptation. He would *not* jeopardize his people or his country to learn the extent of his power as influenced by the Eye of Behelwer. He couldn't risk it.

Maybe one day, he would, but today, while he was in Castle Belmont and could clearly recall the faces of all who worked in his house, Gavin would resist the stone's temptation.

Licking his lips, Gavin forced his tongue to form the words of the protection spell that rejuvenated the province's wards. From the moment he and William had been tasked with seeking the Eye and protecting it, they'd spent every moment contemplating the best way to safely utilize its power. They'd decided to use it to strengthen the protective measures they'd cast over the province and, if possible, extend them to as much of Kordouva as they could.

So far, the Eye of Behelwer hadn't granted Gavin more power than was necessary to safeguard his lands, but it was quickly becoming apparent that the Eye was consuming the magical energy around it from the other artifacts.

Gavin wished he'd had a better and preferably isolated location to keep it, but this was his only vault capable of keeping objects like this.

"I suppose I'll just have to ask William to help and increase the frequency of dispersion," he muttered, gently laying the Eye in its regulatory box. Even that cautionary measure wasn't enough to negate the stone's effects.

The Eye of Behelwer sought power to amplify, and there seemed to be no way around it but to use it wisely.

Gavin shut his eyes. How had this task fallen to him? Jameson was more than capable of looking after the Eye himself, so why wasn't this his burden?

Sighing heavily, Gavin turned on his heels and exited the vault. His temples pounded. Weariness weighed his limbs down. He'd have to rest before he was able to continue on in his day. Gavin smiled. He might even have to miss training the newest recruits this afternoon. He couldn't stand their gawking. He was, after all, only human. Though with the way they regarded him, Gavin feared he'd be mistaken for a god, like the way Darshovians worshiped Penumbra.

He shook his head. His life was utterly absurd. He couldn't wait to grow old and let society discard him as a frail man awaiting death's embrace. Only then would he find peace enough to enjoy the beauty of life.

Chapter Seven

Adelaide

The cool breeze was a welcome kiss on her cheeks. Taking a deep breath of fresh mountain air, Adelaide relished the illusion of freedom as she stepped foot outside of the Belmont's estate for the first time in two weeks. Her veins buzzed with excitement, eager to see her parents for the first time in over three years.

So many times these last few years, Adelaide wished she could change her mind. Every night, she bitterly regretted the day she'd put herself in the same path as the Master of Thieves. If only she'd chosen a different person that day, or hadn't stolen at all, Adelaide wouldn't be in this position. She wouldn't be lying to people who were genuinely kind and friendly toward her, which of course only added to her guilt.

But none of that mattered right now, because if she chose to let it bother her, her parents would know, and they would ask about it and how she was doing. Adelaide couldn't have that. She couldn't let them worry about her when she wasn't the one wholly dependent on a treatment they couldn't afford from a kingdom that Kordouva had shut itself to long ago. If it wasn't for that, Adelaide wouldn't have turned desperate. If it wasn't for the long nights of bargaining with the gods to spare her mother, Adelaide wouldn't have turned to stealing. And if it wasn't for that act of desperation, Adelaide wouldn't have been forced to work for the Master of Thieves.

It was stupid, really. *She* had been stupid.

But then if she hadn't begun to steal and caught Mistress Scrabs's attention, how would her family be now? What would have happened to her mother?

Adelaide shook her head. She couldn't continue to dwell on this. In a year, Mistress Scrabs would allow her to leave her service. In a year, Adelaide could go free and return to her home. She sincerely doubted Mistress Scrabs would stay true to her word, but if Adelaide let that harsh reality sink its claws into her heart, she feared she would not survive as Mistress Scrabs's pawn.

So instead, Adelaide held tight to the idea that her future would be blessed by freedom's embrace. That, and the simple fact that her immediate future was painted by a bright sunset with smiling shades of pink and orange and of a few hours spent with her family. She'd never known what to do with her days off while assigned to other estates in the Master of Thieves's quest to procure rare magical artifacts from the kingdom's wealthy. She'd always been too far away, but now that she was here at Castle Belmont, she could. After all of her underhanded work these last four years, she could finally see her family and judge for herself whether everything had been worth it.

Adelaide twisted a strand of her hair around her finger in thought. Gazing past the fields of squat burbairé trees, Adelaide's eyes saw a world of her own imagination. She feared the longer she stayed at Castle Belmont, the more dangerous her task would become. But in the two weeks she'd been there, Adelaide hadn't been able to figure out how to trigger the faux wall where Archduke Hughes stowed his most treasured possessions. And anytime she'd scraped together her courage to investigate the restricted areas of the castle, someone had sought her out. Their timing was uncanny. If it wasn't Sir Maxwell coming around the corner, whistling, then it was the steward or another of the household's staff.

Then, of course, there were the increasing instances in which she was greeted by Archduke Hughes's presence. Adelaide let her hair unwind itself. The slight curl at the end of her hair bounced as it settled back on her shoulder.

Adelaide still wasn't sure what to make of the White Hawk. The rumors she'd heard of his ferocity in battle and the strength of his magic didn't quite align with the prim and quiet man she'd met. The only thing that seemed to indicate that there was any truth to them was the detached way he'd asked about her wrist. She supposed it was beneath him to ask, but the fact that he had made Adelaide wonder who Archduke Hughes truly was. Maybe he was just misunderstood, or awkward. It couldn't have been easy fighting in Penumbra's War as young as they were. It especially couldn't have been easy for the archduke to take command of the Battle of Rivenfield after Darshovi had decimated Kordouva's capital and killed the royal family.

Surely someone who fought as fiercely to protect their homeland as the archduke had wasn't really lacking a heart. And besides, Adelaide reasoned with herself, the rest of the staff seemed happy and well-treated. In fact, she'd refused a handful of invitations to join Cathy and Juliana on their trip into the city. Even Elizabeth had asked if Adelaide would like to accompany her on her own visit home.

Adelaide smiled. She wished she could stay. Despite the circumstances that had brought her to Castle Belmont, she actually quite liked it there. And the wages were better than what she'd had at other estates.

Passing another field of winter greens, Adelaide's mind came to a halt as the wooden fence, faded from the sun and weather, came into sight. Within its protection sat the house she'd longed to return to.

Grinning at the sight, Adelaide's steps hastened. Letting herself inside the gate, she walked up the front pathway and up the porch stairs. The door opened before she could knock.

"Addie!" Her brother Ethan pulled her into a hug so strong it squeezed the breath right from her lungs. Pulling away, he looked her in the eyes and seemed to study her from head to toe. "What are you doing here?"

"I'm not allowed to visit?" Adelaide teased.

Ethan laughed, welcoming her inside. "We just weren't expecting you, but Amber saw you—"

"It's Addie! It's really Addie!" Amber called. Adelaide braced herself for another fierce hug as her sister came barreling down the hallway, her braided hair flying behind her. Amber didn't let a second go to waste, wrapping her arms around Adelaide and nearly knocking her over. "I *knew* I saw you walking up the road! Ethan tried to tell me it wasn't you, but I knew it was!"

Adelaide laughed as the fiery-haired girl turned a glare on the other. Ethan only took a step away and put his hands up in surrender. "I can admit when I'm wrong, no need to scold me."

"Oh, Adelaide, dear!" Adelaide's heart skipped a beat at how withered her mother's voice still sounded. She curled a hand into a fist by her side. Her nails bit into her palm, giving her something to actively focus on rather than her concern. Even though her mother was being treated with the proper medication, it still wasn't enough. Her mother looked as frail as she had when she'd left. Adelaide shoved the irritation aside. That wasn't true. Her mother was up and walking, albeit with assistance, but she was no longer bedridden, drifting in and out of sleep and a state of delusion. "Look at you! You've grown so much!"

Adelaide turned her face away, hiding her laughter behind a hand. "I don't think I've grown since I was fifteen, Mama."

"That must mean it's been too long since we've seen you," her father added, smiling softly at her as he helped her mother into a seat by the cold fireplace. "How are you? How are you here? I thought..."

Adelaide's smile dimmed, knowing these were all questions she had to answer. Even if her parents knew she was involved in something dangerous, they'd never once let on. Adelaide didn't know how much longer she could tiptoe around the situation. Their ignorance—pretense or genuine—was for the best.

"I'll grab some spiced mahlder," Ethan offered, brushing past Adelaide. As he passed, he whispered, "We need to talk."

Adelaide swallowed and nodded her head solemnly. Tearing her gaze from Ethan's retreating back, Adelaide let Amber lead her to the couch opposite their mother and father.

"Well," Adelaide started, "I never really liked working so far away, so I decided to come home. I missed you all."

Her mother smiled. While her face lacked the vibrancy it once had before she'd fallen ill, Adelaide's mother had greatly improved. Her eyes were brighter than they'd been the last time Adelaide had seen her. "So you're here to stay?"

Adelaide's heart clenched at the hope in her eyes. "I'll be closer from now on. I'm working at Castle Belmont."

"Castle Belmont?" Ethan asked. Adelaide let her gaze fall to her lap at the accusation in his voice. As if shaking the knowledge of why Adelaide was really home from his mind, he added, "Congratulations, Addie. That's a very prestigious position."

"I know," she said quietly. She didn't need to be reminded of that fact, not when the rumors of the archduke's reputation had lived in her head for the last two weeks. Of course Ethan would feel it necessary to remind her of the precarious situation she was in, especially if she successfully stole from Castle Belmont.

Adelaide snapped from her thoughts as Amber begged her to tell her all about the inside of Castle Belmont.

So Adelaide did. She told them of the whimsical patterns of the carpets and the intricate beams that lined the ceiling in the great hall like a blooming flower. She told them of the painted rafters in the breakfast room and the three-story library that held a secret entryway into the archduke's personal chambers.

Captivated by the grandeur of the Belmont estate and its stone castle, her family listened, and the more Adelaide told them, the more her worries lessened as her mind was swept away by the normalcy of it all.

Chapter Eight

Gavin

The late afternoon sun glinted off of her hair, making it look like spun gold as the loose curls bounced with her movements. Gavin wasn't certain if it was guilt rotting in the pit of his stomach or trepidation. If anyone found out he was following a mere maid, a woman of little suspicion, he'd be reprimanded by the Council of Magic for abusing his power.

But if his growing suspicions proved to be true, he'd finally have a way to find Mistress Scrabs and bring an end to her operation.

That's the justification he held on to as he followed Adelaide from the estate. Staying several yards behind her, Gavin didn't know which he would rather be true: that she *was* an agent sent by the Master of Thieves and therefore her thief, or that he was making a complete fool of himself and wasting his magic by invisibly following an innocent woman.

If the latter proved to be the case, he could already hear William chastising him for letting his theories get the better of his rational mind. But if he was right and Adelaide *was* the thief referenced in all of the reports and in his informants' letters, Gavin would finally have the break he needed to make actual progress in putting a stop to Mistress Scrabs's underground markets and maybe even connecting Lady Alyton to the Den of Thieves as the Master of Thieves herself.

It didn't ease the guilt curling inside his gut.

In the two weeks she'd been at the estate, Adelaide hadn't done anything to perpetuate his suspicions. It was certainly possible that she'd only lied about her work experience and nothing else.

Granted, forgery was a crime in and of itself, but it wasn't like her lie had hurt anyone. Or at least, not that Gavin, Thomas, or William could find out about anyway. All of their inquiries had turned up only dust.

And much like their inquiries, if Gavin didn't have time to change before he had to see anyone upon his return to Castle Belmont, the dust of walking along the dirt road would surely give him away.

As it was, he hadn't told anyone of his plan, only that he would be away from the estate this afternoon. He'd refused to elaborate any further, though the fact didn't stop William from hounding him with questions all during their training session this morning.

He didn't understand how a man could talk, fend off attacks, and conjure magic as freely as William could without so much as showing any signs of tiring. Then again, Gavin hadn't either. There was a reason why his cousin had trusted Gavin and William more than even the Commander of the Royal Legion.

The three of them had grown up together, they'd trained together, and they'd managed to survive together. And with their survival, their kingdom had remained intact, even if their late sovereign couldn't be saved.

Gavin remembered the day the moon had eclipsed the sun. The veil between worlds had evaporated, if only for an hour, but it had been enough for Darshovi to conjure the Penumbral Realm's army and overwhelm the palace without ever having to step foot in the heart of Kordouva. While Gavin, Jameson, William, and the forces they commanded waged war at the borderlands, Penumbra's army had assassinated their royal family and decimated the capital city.

It was only when the light of their swords had been extinguished that anyone knew anything was wrong.

But by then, it had been too late.

Despite that, they had survived. The eclipse had ended, and in its wake, Gavin had become the White Hawk of Kordouva for his courage through the dark trial, his cousin had become king as the only survivor of the royal family, and William had steadfastly refused the position of Commander of the Royal Legion in favor of serving beside Gavin.

Together, the three of them had restored their kingdom, and ever since, they'd shared the burden of protecting it. But if Gavin's fears concerning the Master of Thieves proved true, and it was power she sought more than wealth, all of their efforts would have been in vain.

And with another solar eclipse on the horizon, Gavin's patience had turned into desperation.

He needed to find the Master of Thieves before it was too late. Just once, Gavin wanted his intuition to be wrong. He knew it was possible that he was utterly fixated on finding the thief, and that he was drawing conclusions where no such evidence existed. Adelaide was calm, elegant, and utterly transparent. Though, Gavin admitted, he didn't quite understand her. Could someone be both open and a mystery? Or perhaps he found her puzzling because the persona she presented was all an act.

If he was right…Gavin wouldn't be terribly disappointed. It wouldn't be the first time someone, or the idea of them he'd conjured in his head, had betrayed him.

Watching curiously as the endless field was interrupted by a worn fence and a small two-story house, Gavin's gaze gravitated back toward Adelaide. Her pace had quickened. He followed suit and hurried to keep up with her.

Adelaide nearly bounced down the path up to the house in her haste. Gavin stayed behind, observing from the gate as a figure in the upper window disappeared. A moment later, the front door opened, and a tall figure pulled Adelaide into a hug.

"Addie!" the man said, excitement buzzing in his astonished voice.

Gavin shook his head and turned away.

So she hadn't lied about that. She really did have relations here. Whether or not he was right in assuming this was her family or if Adelaide was just close to the inhabitants of this household, Gavin knew for certain that he had no right in witnessing their private moments.

What a fool he'd been.

Taking one last glance at the plain house and its chipping porch supports and turned spandrils and trim, Gavin just made out a man helping a woman to a seat in what must have been a sitting room.

Gavin shut his eyes to gather his composure. Adelaide hadn't lied about her family, or her mother's health. His shoulders slumped. He wasn't certain if it was from relief or disappointment. Adelaide hadn't lied about her motivation for coming to Castle Belmont.

But still, Gavin's mind nagged at him. He had to be certain of her innocence before he could move on in his investigation.

Glancing down the dusty lane, Gavin turned and squared himself with the house once more. Lifting a hand, Gavin's magic unfurled and reached out to the house. Passing through the cool windowpane, his magic touched the woman he presumed was Adelaide's mother and examined her. He wasn't well adept at healing magic, but knowing what ailed the woman couldn't hurt. Maybe there was something he or William could do to help Adelaide, regardless of how invasive his actions were.

An icy shock flooded his veins. Gavin's eyes widened. A foul swear leapt from his tongue before he could stop it. Still, he pressed harder. Maybe he was wrong.

The cold didn't recede, and neither did the suffocating darkness that unfurled from her mother's aura.

Gavin's lips pressed into a grim line. Withdrawing his magic, he turned on his heel and took long strides back the way he'd come. His chest tightened. Blind to the world around him, Gavin's thoughts swirled darkly.

Maybe it was as he thought.

Adelaide's mother should have been dead.

Chapter Nine

Adelaide

Long after the day had waned and the moon had risen, Adelaide found herself facing the thing she'd dreaded most: the conversation she'd promised Ethan. With no one left awake to shield her from his questions, Adelaide sighed and dragged her eyes away from the smoldering fire to meet his gaze. His eyes blazed with concern.

"I know what you're thinking," she said quietly, "but I don't have a choice. You know that, right?"

"I don't believe that," he said, sitting next to her so their words wouldn't be overheard. "I know you're worried about Mama, but I think between your wages from working at Castle Belmont and what I make at the smithy—"

"It's not that, not really," Adelaide reminded him.

Ethan sighed heavily, rubbing his temple. "How much longer do you have to do this, Addie?"

"I'll be free next year."

His eyes turned sharp. "You mean if you survive this 'assignment,'" he spat.

"I was hoping you wouldn't make the same assumption I did." Adelaide put her head in her hands. "What am I supposed to do? I can't run away from Mistress Scrabs or fail her task, but I also can't get caught, because if I do…" Adelaide broke off, her throat tightening. Forcing a deep breath into her lungs, she finished, "No matter what I do, it could put us all in danger. I don't know what to do."

Her brother hummed in thought. Adelaide fought to keep her breathing steady as she waited for him to say something, anything. "What's the archduke really like? Have you met him?"

Adelaide blinked. "He's…I don't know. He's the archduke. He has power and is incredibly busy." Adelaide paused, her mind replaying how carefully he'd wrapped her wrist and how the brush of his shoulder against hers had caused her stomach to flutter. The tips of her ears heated. "I mean, I suppose he's…benevolent?"

Ethan laughed. "'Benevolent?' Is that the only impression you have of him? You could say the same thing of a tyrant if you ripple a puddle enough."

Adelaide couldn't stop the small smile that pulled at her lips. Shoving at his shoulder playfully, she said, "All right. I have actually met the archduke a few times now. The first was because I couldn't get out of the road fast enough to not be trampled by his horse and tripped. The others were happenstance, I suppose."

That softened Ethan's glare. "So he's…nice?"

Adelaide tilted her head from side to side. "Nicer than the rumors paint him to be." Wringing her hands together, she added, "I don't know if I could approach him with this, though. I…I'm not comfortable with exposing who I am, not after everything I've done."

Ethan put a hand over hers. "You don't have to do this alone, Addie. Let me help you."

Adelaide shook her head. "You are. Knowing that there is someone here to take care of them is enough, especially if something happens to me. I need you here, Ethan."

Ethan clenched his jaw. Adelaide took his hand in hers and squeezed. "Promise me you won't do anything foolish just because I have."

Adelaide's heart pounded between her ears in the brief silence.

"Fine," he relented, pulling his hand back. "But the moment you need help—"

"I will. I'll absolutely ask for it."

Seemingly satisfied with her answer, Ethan leaned forward and wrapped Adelaide in a bruising hug. "I'm glad you're closer to home at least."

"Me too." Adelaide reluctantly pulled away. "I'll visit as often as I can."

"Mama and Papa will like that." Ethan nodded, walking her to the door. "Are you sure you don't want me to walk with you back to Castle Belmont?"

"I'm sure," Adelaide said, draping her cloak around her shoulders. "It's a full moon tonight. Penumbra can't harm me." Adelaide wagged her finger at him. "Besides, I'm taking a lantern with me, so I'll have plenty of light to see by too."

Ethan shook his head, telling her to wait a moment. Adelaide huffed. She really needed to return to the estate before she lost her will to, because if she stayed the night with her family, she'd want to have breakfast with them, and if she had breakfast with them, she'd be late for her duties, and then she'd lose the position and have to face Mistress Scrabs's wrath once again.

"Here," Ethan said, handing her a sheathed dagger and belt. "Take this with you. It'll make me feel better."

Adelaide slipped the blade from its sheath, testing its weight in her hold.

"What do you think of it?"

"Is it one of yours?" she asked.

Ethan bobbed his head.

"I'm not a weapons expert, but I think it's perfect. It feels like nothing in my hand." Adelaide smiled, fastening the belt around her waist.

Ethan blew out a relieved breath. "I'm glad. I made it with you in mind, and when Master Woodstock saw it, he insisted on imbuing it with magic."

Adelaide frowned. "And he didn't wish to sell it?"

"No."

Adelaide stared at her brother, studying him. Magical weapons were far too precious not to sell, for they both knew the price they could fetch at either legal or illegal markets.

"Just take it, Addie."

"Fine," she sniffed. "It seems we both have our secrets, and I can respect that."

"Good, then so can I."

The frost in Adelaide's veins melted. Wrapping her arms around her brother for one last hug before she left, she said, "I missed you."

"We missed you too, Addie. They'll be so happy when I tell them you'll visit more."

Adelaide didn't respond. She hoped she could survive long enough to keep that promise. So instead, she offered one last farewell and stepped out into the crisp night with only the lantern to guide her way and a dagger she didn't know how to use to defend herself.

Dark shadows writhed all around Adelaide. Her mind conjured shapes and figures from their depths that stalked her progress back to Castle Belmont. The hilt of the dagger Ethan had given her was a minor comfort in her grasp. Wind whipped her hair and howled between the trees on either side of the lane. It hadn't occurred to her to bring any matches with her in case her light was extinguished, as the night had been still when she'd left. Clouds blotted out the light of the moon, wholly extinguishing it. A cold, damp air rolled in down from the surrounding mountaintops. The farther she traveled away from home, the stronger the breeze had become, and a light drizzle of rain warned her of an oncoming storm.

So Adelaide did the only thing she could think of. She began to run. She ran until she couldn't anymore. The cloudy night was too dark for her to be so careless. If she tripped and fell, no one would find her until morning, which was the worst of all the situations her fears had imagined. The next was the idea that she'd have to walk the rest of the way to Castle Belmont with a sprained ankle. Then came the embarrassment of having yet another injury to hinder her in the short time she'd been at the estate.

Besides, it seemed that the rain had been a passing shower, though Adelaide didn't want to risk Penumbra's ire. The night belonged to the parallel realm and its god, favoring those who worshipped its shadows. Adelaide was foolish to venture out into its clutches without any care or contingency.

Her eyes cast wary glances all around her. Adelaide often found herself looking over her shoulder as if she expected someone to be following her.

But there was never anyone there.

A relieved sigh escaped her when she saw the glowing torches mounted on either side of Castle Belmont's gate in the distance. Picking up her pace, Adelaide squinted against the darkness. She was almost there. She could even make out the looming statures of the guards stationed just out of the light's reach. Beyond them, Adelaide could see a bobbing light. Perhaps another sentry or a new pair of guards were coming to relieve their shift. If that was the case, at least Adelaide could tuck that information away for future use.

Another gust of wind tugged at her clothes, pushing at her side. A force knocked into her. The pommel of her dagger poked into her ribs from the force, burning hot through her clothing. Startled, Adelaide dropped the lantern. Much too slowly, her mind caught up to what was happening. A hand clasped over her mouth before she could even let out a breath. Adelaide could do nothing as she was dragged from the lane and into the forest. She squirmed in the man's grasp. Managing to free an arm, she began tugging at his hold on her.

"Stop it," a harsh voice ordered. Adelaide's blood froze. She didn't stop. If anything, the realization that Mistress Scrabs had sent Jeffery after her only made her panic more.

Swearing, Jeffery stopped and spun her around. His hand never even slipped from its place over her mouth.

Fumbling for the dagger in her short-lived freedom, Adelaide's lungs heaved. Adelaide blinked, whimpering as Jeffery slammed her into a tree.

"Not a word, Addie. Understand?"

Adelaide nodded. Her chest burned from the weight of his arm pinning her against the tree. She let her arms fall limply to her side. Her stomach burned. Swallowing down her anger, Adelaide banished the idea of using the dagger from her mind. It would do better to save it for when she really needed it.

"You haven't checked in with us," Jeffery said casually. "Mistress Scrabs was getting worried about you."

"I haven't had time," Adelaide lied, ignoring the concerned claim and hearing it for what it truly was. Impatience. Irritation. A threat. "I'm being watched too carefully at the estate. I have nothing to report."

Adelaide couldn't make out his freckled face in the dark, and she was glad for it. It meant he couldn't see hers very well either. Maybe Penumbra wasn't as bad as everyone made its powers out to be. It was certainly doing her a favor at the moment. If she had to look at his smug face, Adelaide would've stabbed him and been done with the whole affair.

She frowned. Stabbing Jeffery wouldn't patch the dam. The real problem would still be there. Mistress Scrabs would still be alive to command Adelaide and hold her accountable for her debt.

"Is that so?" Adelaide's stomach twisted at the skepticism in his voice. "You certainly had time to visit your family today." Adelaide's eyes widened. She wanted to protest, to beg for their safety, but Jeffery continued, "Maybe you've gotten too comfortable. Or could it be that you've forgotten what you're here to do? Do I need to—"

A bright light flashed out of the corner of Adelaide's eye. Adelaide turned her head against it. The weight of Jeffery's arm lifted from her chest as he was sent flying through the air.

Stunned, Adelaide couldn't move from where she stood, rooted against the rough tree bark. Her chest burned. Old wounds surfaced in her memory from previous accusations of disobedience.

Adelaide's eyes darted over her surroundings, uncertain of what was a threat to her and what could save her. She barely registered what was happening as Jeffery scrambled to his feet and fled. Two people sped by her. Adelaide looked after them, dazed. As the armor-clad feet chased after him, making a noisy ruckus through the woods, Adelaide sagged against the tree. Her mind finally calmed enough to recognize what had happened. Turning toward her savior, she pushed some stammered words of thanks past her lips.

"It seems I keep finding you in predicaments," Archduke Hughes replied calmly. Adelaide's eyes widened. His magic flared at his fingertips, glowing brightly enough to illuminate the diminishing space between them as he stepped closer to her and laid a careful hand on her shoulder. "Are you all right, Adelaide?"

Adelaide's breath caught in her throat. She didn't know how to respond. She didn't even think she was capable of responding as

Kordouva's White Hawk stared at her with such deep concern in his dazzling blue eyes. It was enough to calm and capture her in a trance.

But only for a moment, for when she blinked, her mind waged war against the steady beating of her heart.

The shock receded from her mind, and in its place a new inkling of fear emerged. Adelaide's limbs trembled. How was she to explain any of this without implicating herself?

Chapter Ten

Gavin

Gavin held a hand up as he approached the guards. "There's someone on the estate that shouldn't be."

"What do you mean, Your Grace?"

"The barrier. Someone's entered bearing their own ill ambitions," he explained, studying the darkness beyond the glow of the torches' licking flames. "I'm going to investigate."

"Your Grace, we can't allow you to—"

Gavin's lips quirked in a bemused smile. "Please go on. I'd like to hear what you cannot allow me to do."

"What he meant, Your Grace, was that we would be honored to help in your search of the grounds."

Before Gavin could remind them of his combat skills, his ears pricked at the sound of metal clattering against the gravel path leading to the estate.

"Do you think that's the intruder?"

Gavin shushed them and stepped cautiously through the gate, straining to hear if there was anything more. The rustling of bushes met his ears. Crouching down, Gavin laid a hand flat against the ground. Sending a ripple of magic down the lane, he let it fan out to canvass their surroundings. Nothing but empty air or the fuzzy sensation of the woodland met his magic. Furrowing his brow, Gavin concentrated harder, searching for the wall of warmth that indicated living things. He pushed his magic farther out into the woods and down the lane.

His mind sparked. His magic met a wall of warmth with a narrow gap of cold air between it. It was likely that meant that there were two people, or three at the most. Gavin doubted it. The force of their presence disturbing the wards around Castle Belmont's estate was small. He already knew the intruder didn't possess magic, for if they had, they wouldn't have entered his lands so cavalierly, so whoever they were, they were here for something else.

Withdrawing his magic, Gavin stood and addressed the guards, Dame Beatrix and Sir Aiden. "They're a little way into the woods. One assailant. We'll need to be careful because it seems they've taken someone from the path."

"Do you think it's a robbery?" Sir Aiden asked.

Gavin considered the possibility. "Perhaps."

Perhaps it was as simple as that. His gut nagged at him, knowing exactly what he'd brought to his home two weeks ago. It was too coincidental.

"Standing here won't tell us anything." he said decisively. "I'll lead."

Silently, the trio stalked down the lane. Gavin listened for anything, the telltale rattle of the bushes, of groans, shouts, raised voices, anything that would indicate a fight. But there was nothing. And thanks to the wind, he couldn't even make out the low tones of conspiratorial conversation.

If it wasn't for his magic, they wouldn't have any idea who they would find lurking in these woods.

Dame Beatrix signaled for them to stop. Gavin narrowed his eyes, curious as to what had drawn her attention. Had she seen something in the woods?

She pointed. Gavin's eyes made out a rectangular shape on the ground. He nodded in acknowledgement and approached it cautiously. Stooping to get a better look at it, Gavin's blood cooled. A lantern?

Without much thought, Gavin jumped to his feet and strode toward the wood. A fizzle of magical current rippled through the air as he sent it out in search of his adversary.

The figures hadn't moved. Silently, Gavin wove between the trees.

The two guards trailed behind him. A film flicked over Gavin's eyes as he willed himself to give into the magic that granted him sight. Some said humans shouldn't have such abilities. Gavin knew it was the only reason they still had a kingdom. If they hadn't been able to see through the dark nights ruled by Penumbra, Kordouva would have fallen to the shadows.

As it was, he could feel that inky plague roiling in the undercurrent once more. It had to be related to Mistress Scrabs's Den of Thieves and the impending eclipse. It was the only explanation. Penumbra would rise again—with or without the Darshovians to worship it.

Gavin quickly adjusted to the muted hues of green and deep blue as his magic granted him the ability to see in the dark. He halted as two shapes—two people—pressed up against a tree some way ahead of him came into sight. Neither had heard their approach, too engaged in their conversation to notice.

Gavin didn't dare to draw any closer. Even though he didn't know whether it was a robbery for certain, it was still clear to him that the woman was in danger from the pair's posture. Raising a hand, Gavin drew on his magic. A sharp arrow of magic blasted from his hand, knocking the assailant back and onto the forest floor. The guards rushed forward. Watching the scene unfold, Gavin found himself hesitating. He watched as the assailant scrambled to his feet and fled, chased after by the guards.

With their departure, Gavin's gaze flicked to the woman. Though he fully intended to see after her wellbeing, shock flooded Gavin's bloodstream. He recognized Adelaide despite the distorted colors of his nocturnal sight and was unable to explain the anger that simmered in his gut. He didn't know whether his anger stemmed from the danger he'd found her in, or the fact that it might not have been a dangerous situation for her at all. But upon a closer look, Gavin realized she was trembling.

Adelaide's chest rose and fell as she looked around. He clenched his teeth. He had half a mind to follow after the guards and the man who'd fled. Gavin knew it wouldn't change anything, though. Breaking himself from the spell that had captured his mind, Gavin made his way to her.

Fear and apprehension glowed in her green eyes as they landed on him. She looked stricken, but only for a moment. Any trace of her fear, of her bewilderment, fled as she saw his approach, replaced instead by weariness as she masked any expression. Whether by habit or intention, Gavin couldn't explain the change in her demeanor.

Certain there was more to Adelaide than any of them knew, he became even more determined to find out.

The sting in his eyes fled. Plunged into darkness once more as he let his nocturnal sight fade, Gavin raised a hand. His magic danced on his fingertips like flames so he and Adelaide could see each other. Examining her closely for visible injuries, Gavin tried to keep the suspicions from his voice.

"It seems I keep finding you in predicaments," he tried to tease, but he'd failed to sound humorous. Laying a hand on her shoulder, he asked, "Are you all right, Adelaide?"

Adelaide seemed to shake herself from her daze. She dropped her gaze. "Thank you, Your Grace."

His lips pressed into a thin line. Studying her closely in the light of his magic, Gavin reached for the clasp of his cloak and undid it. He shifted its weight from his shoulders and said, "Let's get back to the estate. I'll have Thomas bring us some warm mahlder."

Wide-eyed, Adelaide glanced up. Her eyes finally met his as he settled his cloak around her shoulders. "I hope you don't mind answering some questions about what happened?"

She shook her head. "I'll try. It happened so quickly, Your Grace.

I don't know how much help I'll be." She glanced in the direction her assailant had fled. "Will they catch him?"

"I hope so." For several reasons, Gavin hoped so. He needed to speak with the would-be assailant and find out if there was any connection between him and Mistress Scrabs. He was also hoping to corroborate whatever story Adelaide told him of the ordeal.

Adelaide nodded. Worry gleamed in her eyes but flickered out as soon as it had come. "I hope so too," she said quietly.

Gavin raised a brow. He couldn't say if Adelaide was lying or if she really wanted him to be caught. There was too much Gavin didn't know, and it drove him to the edge of insanity. Every scrap of information he and William had unearthed was like a puzzle piece. He wished he knew if Adelaide's belonged to the same picture or if she was something else entirely. Perhaps he'd know more if he could question the assailant.

Swallowing, Gavin took a step away. "We should return to Castle Belmont, before it starts to pour."

"I would like that, Your Grace. It drizzled a little on my way back and rained for a bit before, but I was lucky that it didn't storm."

Keeping pace with Adelaide as he illuminated more of the space around them so they could pick their way back to the path without incident, Gavin latched on to the chance to learn where she'd truly come from.

"Did you go a long way?" Gavin tried to sound curious, fearing his voice would give away the fact that he already knew the answer to his inquiry.

Adelaide didn't respond right away. "I suppose. To me it wasn't such a long way. Home is a lot closer than it's been, so I didn't mind the walk, Your Grace."

"And your mother? How is she?" Gavin asked thoughtlessly. As his own words landed on his ears, Gavin's heart clenched. Quickly, he added, "I apologize. I shouldn't have assumed that home meant you saw…or even that I was at liberty to ask about—"

Adelaide laughed, but not nearly long enough for Gavin's heart as he realized how much he liked it. It was mesmerizing, just as rich and lyrical as her singing voice. People didn't usually laugh so freely around him. He was the White Hawk of Kordouva. People tended to assume he was someone to be feared. He never corrected them, wondering if the reputation helped him more than hindered him.

Gavin wanted to make her laugh, just so he could hear it again.

"I'm sorry. I didn't mean to laugh, Your Grace," Adelaide said breathlessly, a weak attempt to stifle her amusement. "I just didn't expect you to remember…" She trailed off. Gavin snuck a glance at her. Her face was shadowed by the surrounding night and the glow of his magic. When she spoke again, Adelaide's voice had sobered. "My mother is doing well, better than I expected actually."

"But?" Gavin found himself prompting.

Adelaide didn't answer. Gavin chastised himself, realizing more and more that he was overstepping boundaries he wouldn't ordinarily overlook.

"I'm worried," Adelaide admitted quietly. After what Gavin had witnessed this afternoon, Adelaide had every right to be concerned about her mother's health. Severillik wasn't so easily cured or treated. It was nothing short of a miracle that Adelaide's mother hadn't succumbed to the illness, given how much of her body it had settled into. It made him wonder once more how she could even be alive. "I don't know how much more I can do for her before…before it finally takes her."

Gavin hummed. Sentiments of sympathy and the urge to offer what little help he could fought against each other in his mind. In the end he said, "I'm sorry."

There truly wasn't much Gavin could do, despite how many throughout Kordouva suffered from severillik. The only known treatment that could curb—if not heal—severillik came from Darshovi.

To make matters worse, it was widely known that the medicine had been developed using Penumbra's dark magic and by stealing souls. His cousin wouldn't hear of trading with Darshovi due to the unethical nature of the medication, even in spite of how their people suffered. Instead, the king had made it his top priority to fund research into an alternate treatment option.

But Gavin knew time and money were running out. Too many of their efforts had ended in failure or were diverted away to combat the flux in illegal activities.

"Thank you, Your Grace," Adelaide whispered, her voice tense. Pausing in the hall, she slipped his cloak from her shoulders and offered it to him. "If you'll excuse me, Your Grace, I'd like to retire for the night."

Gavin's lips threatened to frown. He needed to ask her about the would-be thief. Straightening his shoulders, the archduke studied Adelaide's drawn face. In this moment, she seemed truly delicate. Gone was the poised composure she carried herself with, and in its place was unguarded emotion. Strands of her wavy hair framed her round face. He wanted to twirl the loose ringlet around his finger and tell her she was safe.

Gavin shook his head. What was he thinking? He couldn't afford to have such thoughts. He couldn't be swayed by whatever irrational feelings Adelaide was stirring within him.

"Of course. Come to my office in the morning. We'll talk about what happened then."

Adelaide nodded, offering him a curtsy, and left without another word.

Gavin watched after her for a moment before turning away. Sleep would elude him tonight. Worry, irritation, and curiosity plagued his mind. Rather than head for his bedroom, Gavin donned his cloak once more and stalked through the estate and out into the rear courtyard. Rain *pitter-pattered* against the leaves of the prized fruit trees. The barracks were alight with torches.

"I was just about to summon you, Gavin." William stopped before him, waiting for Gavin to catch up to him before he swiveled on his heel and matched his pace.

"Has he been detained?"

"Yes."

"Good. I'd like to question him myself."

Chapter Eleven

Adelaide

Adelaide stared at the ceiling. Her mind raced. No matter how snugly she tucked the blankets against herself, she couldn't stop the icy shiver that trailed over her body. Jeffery had almost gotten her caught alongside him.

By the time she'd made it back to the servants' quarters, news had already reached them of the intruder on the estate thanks to the stable hand, Jacob. It didn't take them long to figure out that Adelaide was the one who'd been grabbed before the archduke and his guards had found them, and pursued the attacker. From that moment on, Adelaide had to battle a flurry of concern and stamp out their anger.

Cathy's words kept spinning around in her mind.

"The archduke will make certain he won't walk free. Just you watch, Addie."

Adelaide was already certain of it, and her certainty offered no comfort. For once, absolute surety posed a grave problem that made anxiety buzz and flitter through her bloodstream.

What if Jeffery named her? What if he told the archduke and Sir Maxwell everything, about Mistress Scrabs, the Den of Thieves, and her part in the thefts?

The anxiety buzzing in her blood reached a crescendo. Adelaide didn't know if she was actually shaking or if it was merely her fear vibrating against her bones. This could be her only chance to steal the Eye of Behelwer.

Fighting against her every instinct to hurry before she lost her nerve, Adelaide carefully slipped from her bed. She kept one eye on Cathy as she made her way to the door. If she could just make it out of the room and up to the third floor without being caught, Adelaide would be one step closer to securing her safety from Mistress Scrabs. And if she succeeded in stealing the Eye of Behelwer tonight, she could leave Castle Belmont without entangling herself any further into the lives of all who lived here—especially the archduke's.

Adelaide chewed the inside of her cheek. But was that what she really wanted? Did she truly wish to leave this behind? The security of Castle Belmont, and the sense of safety she felt around Archduke Hughes?

Adelaide inhaled deeply through her nose. Staying here wouldn't do her any good. Mistress Scrabs had already sent one enforcer after her. No one, not even the White Hawk of Kordouva, could protect her from the Master of Thieves.

Her stomach twisted at the realization. She had no choice. She never had.

Adelaide stepped out into the hall and closed the bedroom door behind her. Looking both ways, she headed toward the main parts of the estate.

Her throat tightened with every step. The assumption that the archduke and Sir Maxwell would both be preoccupied with questioning Jeffery couldn't ease her mind. Not even the vain hope that all of the other guards charged with protecting the Belmont estate would be too distracted to notice her breaking into the hidden room on the third floor. But if Jeffery had already named her as an accomplice…

Adelaide froze. If she was caught now, she'd never be able to deny his accusations. If he'd already told the archduke and Sir Maxwell, and they went looking for her and couldn't find her where she should be, Adelaide would never be free again.

And then her mother wouldn't receive her treatments, and everything she had done would have been for nothing.

And she would still be indebted to Mistress Scrabs.

She'd already witnessed such cases of other *assets* who'd found themselves at the mercy of Mistress Scrabs's damnation. Adelaide couldn't afford to get caught.

Worst of all, Adelaide didn't want to imagine what would happen when the archduke realized who she was and why she'd come to his estate. She didn't want to learn if there was any truth to the rumors whispered about him and his time on the battlefield. He'd been so kind to her, and she'd lied to him, to all of them. Adelaide swallowed. It was just that. She relished his kindness.

Letting her head fall back, Adelaide closed her eyes. She couldn't believe that she had to let this opportunity go. It would be safer if she did, even though she sincerely doubted another distraction would pull Archduke Hughes's attention away like this again.

The only other thing that could possibly draw his attention away would be a summons from the king. But that wasn't likely to happen anytime soon. Kordouva was at peace, and Penumbra was at rest. Darshovi didn't have the strength to raise its hand against the kingdom without the eclipse to bolster them, and she doubted very much Penumbra had the strength or inclination to bargain with them again.

Watching her feet, Adelaide forced herself back to bed. She'd simply have to wait. That was her best chance. She'd also need to get some sleep tonight because she'd have to wake early in the morning if she intended to send word to Mistress Scrabs about what had happened. She'd also need her wits about her for when she met with the archduke.

Adelaide drew the covers up to her chin.

What lie could she possibly tell him that he would believe? Or was it better to keep things simple and wait to see what it was that he knew about the incident first? Adelaide turned on her side, staring at the wall. Her heart twisted. She didn't want to lie. The archduke had proven himself to be the farthest thing from the image she had of him in her mind. He listened, and he seemed to care in spite of how stiffly he acted. Archduke Gavin Hughes was nothing like the rumors made him out to be, and certainly nothing like the other heads of state she'd worked for under the direction of Mistress Scrabs.

Gavin Hughes didn't deserve to be deceived. Adelaide curled up and tucked her arms close to her chest. But would he understand the truth? Could he help her? *Would* he help her?

After all she'd done, Adelaide didn't think she deserved it. She was only grateful she had the ability to help her mother. That was going to have to be enough to soothe her heart.

By the time the pale morning light filtered through the window,

Adelaide was as lost as when she'd returned to her bed. There wasn't any space for relief in her heart that the archduke and Sir Maxwell hadn't come for her last night—that Jeffery hadn't exposed her role as the Den's thief…yet. Adelaide was too consumed with what lay ahead of her. Between her meeting with the archduke and needing to send word to Mistress Scrabs without being caught, Adelaide found herself wishing Jeffery *had* revealed her as the Den's thief. It certainly would've eased her conscience. Now she had to develop a lie and hoped that whatever she said aligned with what Jeffery might've confessed.

Adelaide rubbed her eyes. It was much too early for any of this, especially after the night she'd had. She couldn't meet the archduke with a cloudy mind. She had no choice in the matter, and would have to make do with patience and what little part of the truth she could tell. That was the only way she thought she'd be able to guarantee her safety.

But first, she'd have to send word to Mistress Scrabs. As she dressed quickly, Adelaide hoped she'd be able to sneak off of the estate before the bulk of Castle Belmont's inhabitants rose.

Adelaide spared a glance over her shoulder as she pushed the door open. The tavern's windows were still dark, but she knew without a fraction of doubt in her mind that Dylan was there. Dylan was always there. The Hawk & Thorne Tavern was his station, and one of many of Mistress Scrabs's depots.

Information, artifacts, money, people, whatever she found to be of use to her operation, Mistress Scrabs made certain it was available to her. The Den of Thieves was the quickest way to relay Adelaide's message to her, and ensure it wasn't intercepted.

Stepping over the threshold, Adelaide swallowed. The door swung shut with a *thump* and the *jingling* of the bell. The odor of stale alcohol and an old fish dinner turned her already knotted stomach. Quick footsteps pounded down the stairs.

"We're closed to—" Dylan came to a stop on the stairs, his head nearly even with the overhang of the second floor. His eyes sparked when he realized it was only her. Slowly, he finished his descent and closed the gap between them. "Oh good, you've saved me the trouble of fetching you. The Master of Thieves wanted to see you."

"Mistress Scrabs is here?" Adelaide's hand froze over the bow keeping her cloak around her shoulders.

"Best not to keep her waiting, Adelaide." Dylan's eyes roved over her skeptically. "What did you come here for anyway?"

Adelaide blinked in an attempt to recover her wits. "I had a message for the Master. Jeffery has been detained by the archduke."

"We're aware." Dylan frowned. "I can't say I'm personally upset by the news, but…"

Adelaide took a breath. "Mistress Scrabs is."

Dylan nodded. "Good luck, Adelaide. She's in my office."

Adelaide nodded.

Wordlessly, she crossed the spacious room, weaving between tables as she did, if only to delay the inevitable rather than taking the clear path in front of the counter. Taking a breath, Adelaide placed one foot in front of the other until she'd mounted the stairs and could go no farther. It took all of her willpower to ignore the tremble in the tips of her fingers. She refused to show Mistress Scrabs her fear.

Adelaide glanced either way down the hall as she crested the staircase. The corridor was long and lined with closed doors. Only one way had a door at the end of the hall. The other had a window with lacey curtains parted to the side, exposing the gray dawn. Adelaide turned left and kept a steady pace to calm her nerves.

A firm voice met her knock.

Mistress Scrabs stood with her back to the door. Adelaide squinted against the light that outlined the Master of Thieves, wishing she wasn't staring directly into the sunrise.

"You've been difficult to get a hold of, dear Addie." Mistress Scrabs turned, her half mask gleaming in the sunlight, and gracefully sat in the chair at Dylan's battered wooden desk, crossing her legs one over the other. Placing her hands over her stomach, the Master of Thieves sat back. Her smugness made the shabby office feel like something more, like it was her own office back at the Den of Thieves with its ornately carved trim and richly stained desk. "And now I'm to learn of poor Jeffery's capture from an urchin instead of you. How can you explain yourself, Addie?"

Adelaide tried to smooth the ruffles in her mood, irked by the use of a nickname reserved for those closest to her—or at the very least, those who were kind to her. Instead, she offered the note she had written during the restless hours when sleep had eluded her. "I came to deliver this message to you, explaining that Jeffery had been captured by Archduke Hughes's men and—"

"I'm well aware of that *fact*," Mistress Scrabs spat, her voice full of venom. Closing her eyes, the Master of Thieves took a deep breath to compose herself. Adelaide pressed her lips together. In appearance, Mistress Scrabs wasn't formidable. But her mind, her words, her quiet cunning, that's what made her so dangerous. Adelaide needed to tread carefully, but it seemed as though the Master of Thieves had already condemned her. Even though the tension in her voice had dulled,

Mistress Scrabs's words weren't any less accusatory. Her glare glinted like a knife's edge. "What I want to know is why? How? If you hadn't been so elusive and worried me so, Jeffery wouldn't have been caught, now would he?"

"I had every intention of reporting to you as agreed, but… Castle Belmont is too guarded. I've located a place where the Eye might be held, but haven't been able to confirm its whereabouts. I was hoping to find out before I had to deliver my update," Adelaide explained, vainly attempting to keep the annoyance from her own voice. As an afterthought, she added, "My Lady."

Mistress Scrabs clicked her tongue. Uncrossing her legs, she placed her clasped hands on the desk and leaned forward. "Are you insinuating that Jeffery's capture is my fault?"

"No, My Lady," Adelaide said, "I only meant to explain my tardiness."

"For such a smart young woman," Mistress Scrabs started, standing slowly, "you can't seem to remember your place."

Adelaide followed Mistress Scrabs with her eyes. Her skin tingled with a phantom pain, a reminder of what the woman before her was capable of. Mistress Scrabs came to a stop in front of her and smiled dangerously. Reaching a hand up, Adelaide flinched. Mistress Scrabs's quiet tone was too sweet, a false impersonation of endearment. "As it is, I can't let this go unpunished."

Before Adelaide could take a step back or run from the room, the Master of Thieves had laid her hand on her cheek. Fire licked at Adelaide's bones. Her body went limp as pain sparked through every part of her body and down every nerve. Mistress Scrabs quickly shifted her hand to hold the back of Adelaide's head as her body betrayed her and crumpled to the floor. A scream bubbled up in her throat, but cut off as Mistress Scrabs's magic clawed around her throat and silenced her.

Adelaide's mind went blank. She stopped fighting and just let her body succumb to the fizzle of Mistress Scrabs's magic. Inky black bubbles dotted Adelaide's vision. A flood of exhaustion overcame her. Stars sparked as her vision turned hazy and Mistress Scrabs became a blurred figure above her.

Finally, the Master of Thieves let her go. Her head smacked against the hardwood floor, a dull pain compared to the force of Mistress Scrabs's magic sweeping through her. The pain stopped instantly. Adelaide's heart pounded against her chest. She breathed heavily, heaving in air as though she hadn't ever had enough. Slowly, the shadows faded from her vision, and her eyes cleared. Adelaide's ears rang. Feeling returned to the tips of her toes and fingers, and then throughout the rest of her body.

"There's been a change of plans," Mistress Scrabs informed her, though Adelaide didn't understand her words. A thick fog misted her brain. The Master of Thieves's face had hardened, a rare crack in the airy composure she kept. "I need you to steal something more from Archduke Hughes than just the Eye."

Adelaide groaned, letting her eyes fall shut. Did Mistress Scrabs even realize she couldn't understand a word she was saying?

Apparently not, for the Master of Thieves kept speaking. "I want you to steal his heart. I need the archduke distracted, and if you have his heart, maybe you'll actually be able to get me what I want. You can do that for me, can't you, Adelaide?"

Adelaide swallowed her shame. Tears pricked her eyes. Unwilling to meet Mistress Scrabs's gaze as she crouched beside her and stared down at her, Adelaide instinctually whispered, "Yes, My Lady."

Mistress Scrabs smiled, a chilling expression that did not meet her eyes or soothe Adelaide's soul. The graceful façade restored itself as Mistress Scrabs stood. She straightened her fine silk blouse and adjusted the ring on her finger without an apparent care. "Good. Then I'll leave you to your work. I have more important matters to attend to in the meantime, but by the half-moon, the archduke had better be so in love with you that one little word could influence him. Make the kingdom's shield fall in love."

The Master of Thieves stepped over Adelaide. She had half a mind to grab the woman's boot and drag her down to the floor. But Adelaide could hardly twitch her fingers, let alone command her arms to move or control the whole of her body's strength.

She wished she'd brought the dagger Ethan had given her. Maybe then she would have been a bit braver.

The door closed with a *thump*. Adelaide shut her eyes. Taking a deep breath and then another, Adelaide forced herself up on an elbow. Her mind spun. Closing her eyes against the throbbing of her temples, Adelaide pulled herself to sit up against the wall.

Slumped against it, she waited for the pounding of her heart to subside.

As the *clip-clop* of horses' hooves and calling merchants reached her ears from the streets below, Adelaide forced her mind to make sense of Mistress Scrabs's command.

She wanted her to steal Archduke Hughes's heart?

Did she mean that in the literal sense?

No, Adelaide remembered. She wanted Adelaide to make the archduke fall in love with her.

Adelaide pressed her hands against her eyes and drew her knees to her chest. How was she supposed to accomplish that? She was forgettable, someone who went unnoticed, a ghost.

The archduke would never fall in love with her, especially not as quickly as Mistress Scrabs presumably expected. He was too smart, too insightful. Moreover, Adelaide would never get close enough to him to even attempt to flirt or…

Her blood ran cold.

What if it wasn't flirting Mistress Scrabs expected of her? What if mere words weren't enough to make the archduke fall in love with her so she could steal the Eye of Behelwer?

Adelaide was guilty of many things. And though she hadn't been able to live with that guilt, she realized it was more tolerable than what was expected of her now.

She could not—*would not*—steal someone's heart. Even if she was capable of such a thing, Adelaide didn't think she could allow herself to give such an intimate part of herself.

She needed to find another way. She had to—Adelaide lifted her head.

She needed to put her faith in someone more powerful than herself in spite of how terrifying the prospect was.

Chapter Twelve

Gavin

Gavin stared at the pendulum swinging back and forth with each *tick-tock* of the clock. Adelaide should have been there by now. The sun had already risen, and, if he had to guess, Castle Belmont was bustling with activity.

Had she forgotten?

He shook his head. He doubted Adelaide could have forgotten the events of last night. Being assaulted wasn't something so easily forgotten, and while he'd seen far worse sights—had personally experienced far worse circumstances—Gavin himself hadn't been able to sleep thanks to the inquiry of his own mind. He *needed* to know why, why her, why last night, why any of it.

Tapping his fingers against the desk, Gavin turned the assailant's replies over in his head once more. More importantly, his mind replayed the man's mannerisms. The flickering eyes, the wide-eyed fear, the backtracking. None of it made any sense.

And then there was Adelaide to consider.

Could her disappearance have something to do with what happened last night? Was Gavin right to assume she was Mistress Scrabs's thief?

"*Coopenell,*" Gavin whispered, waving his hand in front of the hidden drawer of his desk. The lock *clicked,* and the drawer popped open, allowing Gavin to grasp the edge and slide it out the rest of the way. He took up his notes and sat back.

There was at least one woman involved in Mistress Scrabs's enterprise, aside from the Master of Thieves herself. A woman who appeared as a maid and disappeared alongside the various artifacts. A woman with green eyes, or possibly gray, and a quiet disposition. A woman incapable of leaving an impression…

Adelaide's eyes were in fact green. The only other thing he knew about her that mattered in this sense was that she herself didn't bear any ill intention toward Castle Belmont, but if she worked for someone who did, the barrier wouldn't discern that. The latter he knew only because she hadn't triggered the wards protecting the Belmont estate. Despite the fact that her arrival at Castle Belmont was suspicious seeing as it coincided with his returning with the Eye of Behelwer, Adelaide had successfully stepped over the protective measure without issue.

Her assailant had not.

The archduke rested his head against his hand.

How many instances could seriously be mistaken for happenstance before it was realized that they were a pattern, or some twist of fate?

Drawn from his thoughts by a soft knock at his office door, Gavin straightened. Sliding the papers back into the drawer and shutting it, Gavin drawled, "Enter."

The door opened slowly. Adelaide stepped into the office and glanced about before her eyes finally landed on Gavin sitting at his desk.

"Adelaide," he said, calmly standing and motioning toward the couches, "please, take a seat."

She nodded and shut the door behind her carefully, her movements sluggish. Gavin watched her curiously. As he drew closer and sat on the couch opposite her, Gavin studied the slight downturn of her pursed lips. He noticed the hitch of her breath as she nearly collapsed and the flash of pain in her emerald eyes. His curiosity gave way to concern.

Adelaide had hardly settled on the edge of her seat before he asked, "Are you all right, Adelaide?"

Her face went slack, her lips parting slightly as if the question had caught her off guard. "Yes, Your Grace. I just had a difficult night's sleep is all."

Gavin doubted that was the whole truth. Crossing a leg over his knee, he hoped his appearance was casual and relaxed, not revealing the tension coiling in his blood. Unfurling his magic out toward Adelaide, he said, "I can imagine. Not many peo—" Gavin's blood froze. His power flared and reared back against the shock of magic that emanated from her. It was like a scar against her soul, one Gavin certainly hadn't expected to encounter. A scar that ran deep enough that the only explanation possible for it was that it had been reopened again and again. Rage boiled in his blood. The urge to ask who had done that to her overcame him.

Gavin coughed, clearing his throat. He couldn't ask that, not without needing to explain how he knew what he did. "Sorry. What I meant was that I don't think many people would be able to forget that so easily."

Adelaide hummed. Her eyes strayed, taking stock of the office.

"Adelaide," he started slowly and leaned toward her, "what happened last night?"

Truth be told, Gavin didn't care about last night. Not anymore. What he wanted to know was what happened this morning to cause the shadows in her eyes that hadn't even been there last night after she'd been attacked.

Adelaide shifted on the couch. "It all happened so quickly," she said quietly. "I was just walking back to the estate. I could see the gate." Her eyes withdrew, misted over by the memory. "And then I was being grabbed. It was so fast, I couldn't even scream for help…I didn't even think to fight. I just…froze. I've never been so terrified, Your Grace."

She'd wanted to call for help? Gavin smoothed his hand against his knee to keep from making a fist, trying—and failing—to tamp down the anger simmering in his gut. There wasn't anything he could do that he hadn't done, or at least, not until Adelaide told him something. "Did he say anything, ask you to do something, threaten you?"

Adelaide shook her head. Glancing down at her lap, she stated more than asked, "I heard he was caught."

"He was," Gavin replied, watching for any indication that could help him gauge her thoughts. "Sir Maxwell is still looking into the information shared with us. The estate is perfectly safe again."

"I'm happy to hear that, Your Grace," Adelaide sighed. "Was there anything else you wanted to ask me about last night?"

Gavin shook his head. An idea sparked in his mind. "No, that was all. I do have one other question, though. What do you know about the Belmont estate?"

"I'm afraid not much, Your Grace." Adelaide's brows drew together.

He offered her a small smile. "A strong magic protects it. Those who willfully bear ill intentions against Castle Belmont or its inhabitants cannot pass through the wards undetected."

"So..." Adelaide tilted her head. "Someone couldn't enter the estate if they meant to do harm?"

"Not technically. It's like an alarm, like the warning bells on the watchtowers."

"Oh."

"You're perfectly safe here, Adelaide. And if it would help, someone could escort you the next time you wish to visit your family, or leave the estate."

"Thank you, Your Grace." Adelaide's lips pulled into a small smile that didn't reach her eyes. "That's very generous of you."

"I take care of my people," Gavin said without hesitation. Shock flitted through Adelaide's widened eyes. Gavin scrambled to explain what he'd meant by the statement, only to be met with a mind that fumbled for words. "I didn't mean to imply that...I only meant that...I do not think of the house's staff, or anyone, as possessions."

Adelaide gave a small laugh. The tension in Gavin's heart eased, and he found himself smiling. "That's not how I took it, Your Grace. I heard it as someone who cares for those around them. I...I've never been in a place where someone cares about even the…lowest stations of their household."

"You would tell me," Gavin found himself saying. His heart thudded against his chest. The rapid beat echoed in his ears as his mind finally realized what his tongue was saying. But Gavin didn't stop himself. "If someone hurt you, right?"

Adelaide tensed. Panic flashed in her eyes. "O-of course, Your Grace."

"Then who hurt you, Adelaide?" he pressed, leaning forward. "And please, don't lie. I know you're hiding your pain. You've been hiding a grimace and a flinch since entering the room."

"You said you take care of your people," Adelaide replied slowly. Her chest heaved. Gavin studied her anew. Curiosity licked at his blood. This woman had no trouble meeting his eyes for simple conversation, but now that he'd asked about her specifically, her gaze had dropped. Was she ashamed? Did she not like talking about herself?

Why couldn't she meet his eyes now?

Or was it that she was hiding something?

"Does that mean you would care for them even if they'd betrayed you?"

Gavin's blood went cold.

Chapter Thirteen

Adelaide

Adelaide fought to keep herself from trembling. Her eyes stung. Everything in her begged her to run, to expel the energy bubbling up inside of her. But she stood firm against the nerves that waged war over her mind.

She couldn't do as Mistress Scrabs had ordered. Archduke Gavin Hughes wouldn't be swayed by a mere commoner—a thief—so easily. And Adelaide couldn't stomach the idea of deceiving someone like that. Petty theft was something she could forgive herself for with time. But making someone fall in love with her?

She would never forgive herself for that, and frankly, she had more self-respect than that. She couldn't—she *wouldn't*—bend her will to go against her own heart.

Adelaide steeled herself against the question she was about to ask—and hoped it was enough to protect her from the archduke's answer.

"Does that mean you would care for them even if they'd betrayed you?"

Adelaide held her breath. She didn't dare look at Archduke Hughes. She forced her hands to remain still and set them on her aching knees.

She had the archduke's undivided attention. From the moment she'd stepped into his office, he'd been studying her.

Archduke Gavin Hughes had lived up to his reputation in that one respect. He was indeed fiercely protective, just as he was kind instead of cold, and attentive instead of indifferent. He'd proven that last night, and just now with his promise to take care of those he considered under his banner.

"In what way," he started, his voice oddly calm, "do you feel you've betrayed me, Adelaide?"

Adelaide shut her eyes so she wouldn't have to see the archduke's reaction. She couldn't keep her silence any longer. "I was asked to steal from your estate…and from you."

"By who?"

Adelaide shook her head. How had she convinced herself that she could remain unscathed even after she told the truth?

"Adelaide." Fabric rustled. Adelaide opened her eyes and watched apprehensively as the archduke walked around the coffee table to sit beside her. He laid his warm hand over top of hers. She savored the warmth even if she didn't believe any comfort would come of the contact. "Who hurt you? Was it the person who asked you to steal from me?"

She swallowed. "Yes, Yo—"

"Gavin," he interrupted. "Please call me by my name. I can't stand titles."

Adelaide blinked, slowly lifting her gaze to find the archduke's intense blue eyes on her. She nodded against her will, lost in the landscape of his eyes and the open concern masking the controlled rage of his features.

"If I tell you," she said slowly, "can I help bring them to justice?"

Gavin raised his brow. "Surely your testimony would be enough?"

"I'm afraid it's much more complicated than that. They're very… powerful," she explained. She fought to force the memory of what happened earlier this morning from her mind. She couldn't let that consume her once again. Adelaide needed to focus, and the way Gavin Hughes was looking at her didn't help her mind clear.

She didn't know someone could look at another person in that way, with such softness and undivided attention. It made her breath catch, wondering if she was all he saw. His gaze made her feel like the only thing left in the world. Adelaide had never imagined that someone would look at her with such compassion. She was a thief. She didn't deserve such courtesy.

"No matter what," Gavin said, an edge to his voice, "I doubt they're more powerful than me. They will be brought to justice."

"I hope you're right," Adelaide murmured. "The Master of Thieves has spent years collecting magical artifacts, Your—Gavin. Her magic is...quite volatile."

Gavin's jaw twitched. He stood abruptly from the couch. A cold draft settled over Adelaide's hand.

She watched helplessly as Gavin began to pace the length of the seating area's carpet.

"We'll need to proceed carefully," Gavin said, "and..." He froze, motion and speech abandoned by some unknown realization. Turning to face her, Gavin's features had softened. Adelaide marveled at how quickly he'd gone from deep in thought to concerned again. "Adelaide, would you be uncomfortable if I included William in this matter?"

"I..." Adelaide wracked her brain, sorting through her feelings. She didn't fully understand what had prompted her to share her plight with the archduke, but she trusted him. Did she trust Sir Maxwell too? Adelaide knew the more people involved in her predicament, the more likely it was that Mistress Scrabs would discover her betrayal.

But Sir Maxwell was Gavin's second-in-command.

"I would appreciate Sir Maxwell's help."

"We don't have to include William if you're not ful—"

"No, I want to. Mistress Scrabs and her Den of Thieves has a lot of influence over Kordouva."

Gavin nodded. "Let me call William into this meeting. Would you like lunch, Adelaide? I fear we might be here for a while."

Lunch?

Adelaide pressed a hand to her empty stomach. She didn't know whether or not she could accept such an invitation, though she was tempted. Adelaide pressed her lips together.

Still, she had yet to see to her assigned duties within Castle Belmont.

"No, thank you," she sighed. Disappointment plagued her mind. Surely the archduke understood her position. "I really must get to work, Your Grace."

The archduke froze. His hand hovered over the window lock. Adelaide arched her brow curiously as Gavin turned to look at her, his lips drawn in a slight frown.

"Adelaide," he started, his voice thick with confusion, "I'm sorry if I didn't make this clear, but you are no longer a maid in this household."

Adelaide's stomach dropped.

The archduke returned to his task at the window without any further explanation. Adelaide's eyes welled with tears. She ducked her head and tried to blink them away.

The creak of the window's hinges grabbed her attention. Watching the archduke through her lashes, Adelaide didn't understand what he was doing as he reached a hand out the window until sparks of magic erupted from his palm. They carried on the breeze. Gavin didn't waste a moment between the last of the magical trail getting swept away and latching the window once more.

"There," he said, turning back to her. Adelaide turned her head to the side. She didn't want him to see how upset and panicked she was. "That should get William's attention. Now, let's finish our discussion."

The cushion beside her dipped under Gavin's weight. Adelaide's hand clenched around her knee. She didn't dare look at him.

"Adelaide, please understand that I'm not firing you," he explained. "In truth, you were only hired because I'd hoped to attract Mistress Scrabs's attention with the advertisement. I'd already suspected you were lying to us, though had hoped I was wrong. Thomas knew your letter of recommendation from Lord Ventner was forged."

"You knew?" Adelaide whispered. Shock struck her heart. She nearly flinched.

Gavin chuckled. Adelaide didn't see what was so funny about her situation. "Not everything, but enough. Surely you've heard the rumors about me."

Adelaide nodded, still unwilling to look at him.

"I meant what I said earlier." Gavin's warm hand slowly returned to hers. Adelaide didn't pull away, instead allowing him to fully wrap his hand around hers. Adelaide took a moment to steel herself and faced him. "I'll protect you, Adelaide. No matter what, Mistress Scrabs will not harm you again. I will not put you in a position where she has that opportunity ever again."

Adelaide let his words soak into her mind for a moment. His eyes blazed with earnestness, the sort of expression that stole her breath and made her want to believe anything he could possibly tell her. But her gut wouldn't let her. Unwavering trust wasn't something she could give so freely. "Why?"

With his other hand, Gavin hesitantly cupped her cheek. Adelaide could've pulled away, and probably should've, but she didn't. She found that she quite liked the gentleness of Gavin's touches, the warmth of his hands, and the way he watched her so carefully as if he expected her to disappear.

"Do I need any other reason than not wanting to see you hurt again?"

"You hardly know me, Your Grace."

Gavin frowned, obviously irked by the use of his title once more. "And what if I'd like to know you better?"

Adelaide's heart buzzed. Why, she wanted to ask again. She swallowed. The question wouldn't provide her with any decisive answer, so instead she said, "Forgive me, but most people have ulterior motives." Slowly, she leaned away from him and carefully wrapped her fingers around his wrist to pull his hand away from her cheek. "Why would you care to know someone you already know to be a liar? I've already agreed to help you in your investigation, so please, there's no need to…to pretend to care about me."

"I'm not pretending. Though if you truly would rather I stop, I will," Gavin started, his lips quirked in a small smirk. "But to do that, you'd have to let go of me as well."

Adelaide glanced down at their hands. In some way or another, they held each other. Adelaide still hadn't let go of his wrist, and Gavin hadn't let go of her hand.

Her stomach fluttered, and Adelaide found she had no retort. She wished he hadn't noticed.

Thinking about that day in the hallway when he'd caught her singing, the tips of Adelaide's ears burned. She couldn't explain why this instance brought the memory to mind, but it had. And now she had a careful decision to make, one she didn't know what to do with.

Part of her wanted this, the comfort, the surety of Gavin Hughes. But another, more cynical part of herself knew it could never be. Whatever feelings stirred in her heart and whatever feelings Gavin thought he harbored toward her, Adelaide knew their relationship—however it was to be defined—was fragile.

A loud knock at the door saved her from having to respond.

Gavin sighed and dragged his hand away from hers. Adelaide let her hold on his wrist slip, savoring the lingering contact until her hand fell back to her lap. He didn't move as he bade the person at the door to enter the office.

"You called for me, Ga—Adelaide?" Sir Maxwell entered the room swiftly, folders tucked under his arm. His eyes widened, seeing them both on the couch. His shock fled as he composed himself, quickly taking a seat across from them. He kept the folders on his lap, holding them protectively—or to keep them from sliding. Adelaide wasn't positive. Adelaide stared at the edge of the coffee table between them, forcing her mind to organize her thoughts as she'd no doubt have to repeat everything she'd told Gavin.

"Yes," Gavin answered calmly. "I asked you here because Adelaide can help in our investigation."

A shock of ice flooded Adelaide's heart.

Investigation?

Mistress Scrabs's command from earlier that morning flitted through the forefront of her mind. An overwhelming sense of understanding washed over Adelaide, followed by a stab of fear.

Had she played right into Mistress Scrabs's plans by confessing her crimes and asking the White Hawk of Kordouva for help?

Dread wormed its way into Adelaide's veins as she met Sir Maxwell's eyes.

"Oh, really?" Sir Maxwell asked, his gaze fixed squarely on her. Adelaide suppressed a shudder under the intensity of his scrutiny. "Pray tell His Grace hasn't coerced you into aiding us, Adelaide?"

Beside her, Gavin scoffed.

"He hasn't, Sir. In fact, I've deceived all of you," Adelaide confessed. "But I'd like to make it right, if possible."

Sir Maxwell laughed and set the pile of folders on the table. "All right. I'm listening."

Adelaide reiterated to Sir Maxwell everything she'd told Gavin. Every so often, the pair interrupted her account with a question, and then came the hardest part of all.

"How did you become one of Mistress Scrabs's agents?" Sir Maxwell asked.

Adelaide studied her clasped hands. "I fear answering that would only incriminate me further. I can say, however, that it was a mistake that I have regretted every day since."

Gavin's knee touched hers. Softly, he asked, "Is it related to your mother's illness?"

Adelaide let out a slow breath. Her shoulders tensed. She couldn't lie anymore. Lying had only brought her more pain and guilt than she could bear. "Yes." Taking a breath, she explained, "As I've said before, my mother is very sick. My family became desperate for a cure or some sort of treatment to ease her pain, but there were none. My father had spent so much money on doctors and herbalists and mages that we were near penniless. My mother begged him to stop, to remember his responsibilities to my siblings and to me, but it was too late.

"So my brother became an apprentice to a blacksmith and I… work was hard to come by for me. I resorted to pickpocketing in the city for money to pay off our debts." Adelaide went quiet, letting her words sink in for a moment. Quietly, she added, "It was the last time I pickpocketed that Mistress Scrabs caught me in her clutches."

Chapter Fourteen

Gavin

Gavin's mind spun at Adelaide's confession. She had a long history of criminal activity, not all of which could be excused by duress. And seeing as her mother was still alive and able to walk in spite of how much the severillik had spread throughout her body, Gavin had to assume possession of illegal goods or—at worst—smuggling were among her list of crimes.

He shook his head. He'd long been unable to blame the desperate people begging for a cure to severillik. If he had been in the same position as Adelaide, Gavin knew exactly what choice he would make if it was his mother or father who was facing such an excruciating death—even if it meant his own death for being caught.

"How?" William asked. "How did Mistress Scrabs come into contact with you after the pickpocketing?"

Adelaide pursed her lips. "She didn't need to. It was Mistress Scrabs herself that I had stolen from."

Gavin straightened. "Does that mean you know Mistress Scrabs's true identity?"

"I'm afraid not." Adelaide shook her head. "It was rather dark, and she was wearing a hooded cloak. It was Jeffery who caught me and brought me back to Mistress Scrabs. By then, I saw she was wearing a mask."

Adelaide's eyes turned distant. For the first time, Gavin noticed the exhaustion that marred her face, reminding him of her earlier ordeal. Just as he started to inquire if she needed to rest, Adelaide added, "She already knew who I was. The whole thing had been planned. They knew all about my family and my mother's illness and how long I had been stealing. She said I was interfering with her business, because word of my pickpocketing had spread amongst the wealthy and was hurting her business. She said unless I could repay her for the damages I'd caused…she would kill us all."

Gavin sat numbly, listening to Adelaide and her plight. The chilling realization that the Master of Thieves had targeted Adelaide and coerced her right from the beginning made anger curl in his blood. The danger Mistress Scrabs posed was no surprise, but the newly revealed depths of her cunning was. Gavin had anticipated a careful and tricky battle against the master thief and her operation, but he hadn't expected to meet someone worth saving along the way. How many others had been forced into working for Mistress Scrabs?

Was Adelaide's character and her story an exception to those in Mistress Scrabs's employ, or were there more flies trapped in her web than Gavin had realized?

If it proved so, he couldn't imagine how he and William were to untangle the intricate tapestry the Master of Thieves had woven.

"So, it was your life and those of your family that Mistress Scrabs offered you in exchange for…for being her thief?" he asked carefully, his shoulders tensing.

Adelaide nodded. Her fingers curled into fists, crumpling the fabric of her dress skirt.

"Do you think you could identify Mistress Scrabs if you saw her without her mask?" William reached for one of the folders he'd brought with him.

"I don't know," Adelaide admitted. Her shoulders drooped.

Gavin laid a careful hand on her arm. Slowly, she turned to look at him. Her dulled eyes were marred by apprehension and worry. "It's all right if you can't. We're grateful for any information you can offer us. Let's start here for today, and then after you've had some rest, we can turn our efforts elsewhere. Does that work for you?"

Adelaide nodded. Turning her attention back to William, she accepted the folder from him and set it on her lap. Gavin withdrew his hand and gave her some space to study the portraits he'd been sent since becoming the archduke.

Glancing away from the folder as his stomach began to churn at the memory of all the marriage proposals offered to him in the past, he saw William looking directly at him. Gavin forced himself to sit still and appear unbothered under his friend's critical gaze. Meeting his eye, Gavin shrugged in reply to William's raised brow.

William smirked, his eyes shining humorlessly.

Gavin glanced away and rested his chin on his fist, his elbow planted firmly on the arm of the couch in what he hoped was a casual manner. All he had to do was avoid William's silent inquisition while they waited for Adelaide to review the portraits of all the women who'd tried to win Gavin's hand.

Out of the corner of his eye, Gavin saw Adelaide lean forward. She began to spread the portraits out on the coffee table. He didn't know what system she employed as she seemed to sort them, shuffling them about and pushing some aside while she drew others closer. He watched, fascinated, as she silently sifted through them and seemed to come to a conclusion for each and every portrait.

Finally, she sat back with a sigh. "I can't be certain if any of these women could actually be Mistress Scrabs, especially as they all seem to be women of the nobility, but…" She trailed off, biting her lip. Indicating the pile in front of her, Adelaide said, "I think these women look similar to Mistress Scrabs and, to my knowledge, have never been targets of her operation."

Gavin mulled over Adelaide's reasoning. "You know who the Den of Thieves has stolen from?"

"Perhaps not all of them, but I could probably recall the victims of the last four years…or at least the ones I've stolen from personally."

Adelaide's words hung heavy in the study. Gavin didn't know what promises he could make and which he wouldn't be able to keep. He was of the mind that she could be granted amnesty, but would Jameson agree? Or would Adelaide have to serve some sentence for her crimes?

In the end, it was William who spoke. "Don't worry, Adelaide. Your help will not go unappreciated if we manage to dismantle the Den of Thieves and bring Mistress Scrabs to justice."

Adelaide didn't respond, still fixated on the portraits. Gavin wanted to explain them, but couldn't find the words to. It sounded odd, didn't it? That he had not only received these portraits as part of marriage proposals that were more like business dealings than declarations of love, and that he'd actually kept them all? Wouldn't it seem odd? Especially when coupled with the fact that he was now using them to root out his main suspect?

Clearing his throat, Gavin leaned forward and picked up the pile of Adelaide's likely suspects. Sorting through them, he said, "Let's see who we have to investigate further."

Quickly looking over the handful of portraits, Gavin paused, staring intently at the second-to-last one. His eyes flicked to William. William raised his brow. Gavin passed the stack over to him. "Have a look, William."

Gavin knew the moment the same realization came over his friend as he straightened his shoulders and put the portraits back on the table.

Staring up at them all was the portrait of Lady Alyton, Gavin's prime suspect and once a relentless seeker of his hand in marriage and outspoken opposition to Jameson's rule.

"Adelaide," he started, tearing his gaze from the small portrait. Turning to her, he meant to ask what she knew of Lady Alyton and what had led her to add these women to her list of suspects, but he found that Adelaide had fallen asleep. As she sagged against the arm of the couch, it looked like Adelaide had only meant to rest her head but ultimately fell victim to her exhaustion.

Shaking his head of all that he wanted to ask her, Gavin stood quietly.

"What are you planning to do now?" William whispered, following after him.

Gavin shrugged, taking his cloak from the hook beside the office door and carefully draping it over Adelaide.

"Let her rest, I suppose."

William snorted. "You mean to say that *you'll* allow the investigation to take a rest, all because our prime witness fell asleep?"

Gavin frowned. Irritation simmered in the undercurrent of his blood. "Adelaide was attacked this morning. Someone used *statique trosher* against her."

"Did Adelaide tell you who?" William's face paled.

"No," Gavin said, "but I have a few suspicions."

"Of course you do," William teased. He smoothed the imaginary wrinkles from his uniform. Opening the door to leave, William paused. Hesitating in the doorway, he turned back. Gavin arched his brow expectantly. What more could he have to say? "Be careful around her, Gavin. Adelaide has successfully stolen from some of the most secure estates in Kordouva, all without suspicion. If we're not careful, she might just steal your title."

Gavin nearly scoffed. "That's absurd, William. I don't think Adelaide is capable of such a malicious act. She's…"

Gavin trailed off. He didn't know what he intended to say, or how he could possibly be certain of it. Adelaide had confessed to working for Mistress Scrabs, and that she'd been involved in the string of high-profile thefts over the last four years. How could he know what she was or wasn't capable of?

"You care for Adelaide more than because you have a vested interest in her safety as our only firm lead in this case." William smiled wryly, stepping over the threshold.

Gavin's patience waned. Could he slam the door in William's face, or would that only encourage his teasing?

"And if I do?" Gavin reluctantly entertained his friend's notion. "Do you think it would compromise our investigation?"

"I think a better question would be—is it all a ploy?" William countered. "How do we know this isn't all part of Mistress Scrabs's plan to steal the Eye?"

Gavin considered his friend's question. It was a difficult question, not because it was complicated, but because it conflicted with his instincts. It made him wonder if perhaps his judgement wasn't already clouded. Nodding slowly, Gavin said, "Then the best thing we can do is continue to watch Adelaide."

"And how do you intend to do that? We can't have guards hovering around her at all hours," William pointed out.

Gavin pinched the bridge of his nose. "No, I suppose we can't."

William tilted his head. "This is going to sound absurd, but what if Adelaide moved into the archduchess's chambers?"

Gavin froze, nearly gawking. "Why would—"

"It would allow you to keep a closer watch on Adelaide, and…" William held up his hands and took a step out into the hallway, "you two could pretend to fall in love. It would allow you to continue the investigation without treating Adelaide like a suspect or raising any suspicion that she's been discovered or is working with us to dismantle the Den of Thieves. It would protect her from Mistress Scrabs."

Gavin turned the suggestion over in his mind. "It *is* the only room that doesn't have its own entrance or exit. If Adelaide wishes to leave the archduchess's suite, she'll need to go through mine first."

"Do you think we should ask Adelaide before committing to this?"

"No," Gavin said. "If I do, I may not have the resolve to go through with it."

"I'll give the order then," William said as he finally took his leave.

Gavin sighed. His gut churned, wondering if he'd made the right decision or if he'd let William convince him to make a mistake.

Softly shutting the door to his office behind him, Gavin spared a glance back at Adelaide. She'd curled herself up on the couch and tucked his cloak around herself. A slow smile pulled at Gavin's lips. He shook his head. Quietly, he crossed the room to his desk and took up his quill.

Aside from the investigation, Gavin had a never-ending list of state affairs to tend to. He supposed it was better to chip away at his tasks now than to continue allowing them to accumulate.

He wondered if it was too late to abdicate his title.

Chapter Fifteen

Adelaide

Adelaide sat up slowly, blinking. Soft candlelight flickered along the walls, casting soothing shadows that danced against the natural wood tones. The warm blanket fell from her shoulders. The fog retreated from her mind second by second. A slow realization sank into the pit of her stomach.

Nearly vaulting herself off the couch, Adelaide hastily folded the archduke's cloak and turned toward the door.

"Did you sleep all right?"

Adelaide jumped. Swiveling on her heel, Adelaide found the archduke seated at his desk across the room from her. She swallowed against the dryness of her tongue and nodded. "Very well, actually."

"That's good. I'm sure you needed it after the morning you've had." Gavin stood and walked around his desk to lean against it. Adelaide studied him. Her eyes lingered on the way he'd rolled his sleeves up to his forearms, tracing over his scars and scrolling tattoos. The image of a hawk in flight among the thicket of ink enchanted her. "I hope I didn't overstep, but I've asked Elizabeth to have your things brought to the archduchess's chambers."

Lightning struck Adelaide's mind. She forced her attention back to what Gavin was saying. Slowly, her mind processed his words.

He'd what?

Gavin huffed a laugh. He dragged a hand through his slightly disheveled hair, partially pulling Adelaide's attention back to the scrolling artwork on his forearm. Her blood simmered. That heat pooled and curled in her gut. She could hardly focus. Perhaps she needed more rest. "I know. It sounds ridiculous, doesn't it? William and I just thought it would be best, because…"

Adelaide waited expectantly as he trailed off, but no explanation came. "I'm not sure that's…" She paused, considering the idea and all it could possibly entail. By all accounts, it would look as though the archduke had fallen for her. It would buy her time. More importantly, it bought her protection from Mistress Scrabs's wrath. Her eyes raked over Gavin. Oddly, his gaze was intent on the floor. He was even fiddling with the cuffed roll of his sleeves, like he intended to straighten it. Adelaide frowned.

Gavin didn't seem like he thought her living in the archduchess's chamber was a good idea.

Taking a breath, she started anew. "I mean, if you think so, then I'd be happy to. I just think it would be a little suspicious. Why would you move someone like me into the archduchess's suite? Wouldn't that rouse suspicion?"

"It might, and I understand if it makes you uncomfortable. I promise the room will be yours. I won't even step foot in it," Gavin said earnestly, taking a small step toward her. Adelaide held her breath, considering his words. He stopped in his tracks, apparently thinking better of coming near her, and instead appeared to shrink. His shoulders relaxed, and his face softened into an expression of genuine concern. "If you—"

"Thank you," Adelaide said. Her heart slowed. He wasn't lying; that she was sure of. "Though I must admit that wasn't my concern. I…trust you, even if you cannot trust me." She tucked a strand of hair behind her ears. Wrapping her arms around herself, she explained, "I only meant that it would seem odd to other people, and…I'm afraid of what Mistress Scrabs will think when she finds out."

"Oh," Gavin said, his voice on the verge of disbelief. Adelaide offered him a small smile she hoped reassured him of her trust in him. Clearing his throat, Gavin said, "I wouldn't worry about Mistress Scrabs too much. Perhaps this will work to your benefit. She may believe you've stolen my heart instead, providing you with the perfect opportunity to steal what she sent you here for, or at least that's what William said when he proposed the plan."

Adelaide froze. They couldn't know it, but that was exactly what Mistress Scrabs had ordered her to do just this very morning. Stiffly nodding, Adelaide laughed humorlessly. "I suppose you're right."

Gavin narrowed his eyes, cocking his head. "Is that all right? If we—*I*—pretended to court you? It would provide a believable cover for having you stay in the archduchess's suite and for us to spend time together to investigate Mistress Scrabs's true identity."

Adelaide's nerves squirmed. Rationally, Sir Maxwell's suggestion made sense, and Gavin was right. If they pretended to fall in love, it would provide them with the perfect excuse to spend time together. But the idea terrified her.

Gavin had made it so easy for her to forget who he was—and who she was. He made her believe everything she thought of herself was a lie, and if she let herself fall into that dream, Adelaide would be blinded to reality. She couldn't afford that. She couldn't allow herself such follies.

But if they were able to defeat Mistress Scrabs…Adelaide held her breath for a moment. Maybe the scheme wasn't as dangerous. Gavin was the White Hawk of Kordouva, a formidable magic wielder and master swordsman. How could she ever think he wasn't capable of capturing Mistress Scrabs and dismantling the Den of Thieves? Hadn't Adelaide trusted him enough to confess her crimes to him? Wasn't this what she wanted when she came to his office this morning? "Fine, yes. Um, I was just thinking it through. I think it makes sense for us to pretend to be…well, I'm not sure what to call it because 'lovers' is too serious, but that's essentially what we'd be doing, isn't it?" Adelaide nearly laughed at the idea. The air in the room was much too thick. Adelaide cleared her throat and brought her focus back to Gavin. Smiling slightly, she hoped to ease the weight on her chest before it caved in. She needed more air, or space, or something to alleviate the pressure building up between them.

She wondered how Cathy and Juliana would react when they learned she'd be staying in the archduchess's chambers. Would Castle Belmont's staff treat her differently? Would they treat her like a mistress or like an archduchess?

With any luck, Adelaide hoped, she wouldn't see anyone and could avoid whatever awkwardness might come of this development.

"If we're going to go through with this plan, I…well, I'm not sure. What is it exactly I should be doing?"

"Whatever you want." Gavin spread his arms. "Castle Belmont is at your disposal. Do as you wish. I'll come and find you once I'm done with this paperwork, and our ruse can begin."

"All right," Adelaide agreed, "then perhaps I'll walk the gardens. I've heard how beautiful they are."

"They truly are. My mother took great pride in them. I've done the best I can while her and my father are away by the coast, but I don't have much of an eye for shrubbery or flowers."

Adelaide suppressed a laugh. "I can imagine. It's quite a large space to fill. It must be difficult to craft a plan that has blooms year-round yet still looks tasteful throughout the year."

"It is, especially since I had wanted to put an emphasis on plants that were useful to us in tonics and for their magical properties."

"Were you able to do that?"

Gavin shook his head. "Nothing I proposed fit into the plan well, and in the end, I couldn't bear to change my mother's prized gardens."

Adelaide smiled, glancing away and toward the large window. "I couldn't imagine. It would be like trying to fix one of my mother's quilts. I wouldn't be able to do it for the fear I'd ruin the whole thing."

Gavin chuckled, "So you understand my plight then."

"Absolutely." Adelaide rubbed her arms. Studying her feet, she tried to ignore the heat burning the shell of her ears. She liked this. It was normal. There wasn't any threat sowed into Gavin's words or nefarious plots that she would be forced into participating in. There was only laughter and light conversation, just two people getting to know each other. She craved for it to last.

Maybe pretending wouldn't be horrible. Maybe they'd both enjoy it and could become friends. Adelaide's soul tensed. Gavin Hughes was an archduke. Any friendship formed between them wouldn't last. She had to remember that.

"I should go," she said quietly. Bitter disappointment curled up in her gut and settled there like a lead weight. "And leave you to your work."

Gavin slouched, sighing. "If you must. Truth be told, I'm not too eager to return to my stack of paperwork."

"The sooner you finish, the sooner you won't have to worry about it anymore."

"That's one way to think about it." Gavin grinned. Slowly retreating back to his desk, he continued, "The other is that the sooner I finish with this pile, a new one will take its place."

"Even if that's true, why not hold the rose rather than the thorns?" Why would anyone trouble themselves with such negative thinking or the harsh truth of reality?

"I'll have to try that, especially if we're to pretend to fall in love. It would seem odd if I wasn't eager to finish my work, wouldn't it?"

"I suppose it would," Adelaide said slowly. Latching onto the idea stumbling through her mind, she lightly ran her finger down Gavin's cloak draped over the back of the couch, feigning innocence. She kept her voice light and playful. "Just think—the sooner you finish, the more time you'll get to spend with me, the woman you've fallen *madly* in love with."

Gavin didn't laugh. Her heart pounded against her chest. Had she made a mistake? Did he not appreciate the humor of her joke?

"I quite like that idea." His voice was so soft Adelaide wasn't sure if she'd heard him properly. "I'll do my best to meet you in the garden. I shouldn't be too much longer."

Shock settled over Adelaide. All she could do was nod. Without a word, Adelaide let herself out of Gavin's office and numbly wove her way through the estate and out into the gardens before she realized she had nothing to keep the chill at bay but her long-sleeved dress.

Chapter Sixteen

Gavin

The stark ink of the trade proposal Gavin was supposed to be reading went unread. His mind was too busy trying to decipher the flash of emotion that had come over Adelaide at his parting words.

Had he said something wrong? All he'd promised was to meet her in the garden, so why had she gone speechless? It was her idea.

Gavin huffed. Tossing the paper down on his desk, he rubbed his eyes. The proposal would be there tomorrow. Right now, there was something far more important that demanded his attention. He couldn't explain why he gravitated toward Adelaide. Gavin supposed it was because she offered him something no one else could: a way to get close to Mistress Scrabs.

But if he dug a little deeper into his soul, his mind turned over the idea that maybe William had been right.

He was falling for Adelaide.

Right from their very first meeting, he'd been intrigued by her. She was a mystery he wanted to solve. And maybe that wasn't the right way of putting it, but it was the best way Gavin knew to explain his feelings. He wanted to unravel her and see who Adelaide was, the woman the world didn't get to see. Gavin longed to know who she was when she wasn't guarding herself and playing a part in Mistress Scrabs's operation.

Who was Adelaide when she was happy? Who was Adelaide before such sadness had seeped into her life?

That's the woman Gavin wanted to know. Not the one he'd met that day on the road, or the woman who'd been threatened by one of the Master of Thieves's worthless grunts, or the woman who'd been tortured by *statique trosher*.

He wanted to know Adelaide.

Decisively, Gavin stood with a lightened heart. These documents could wait. The lonely woman strolling through the gardens couldn't.

And if Gavin was honest with himself, he needed a break too. For as long as he could remember now, he hadn't had a moment's rest. Ever since Penumbra and Darshovi had been defeated, he'd been busier than ever. Even more so when his parents left for the coast and put Castle Belmont in his care.

His life had been nothing but paperwork and errands for his cousin that allegedly held the sovereignty of their kingdom in the balance. It was a horrible life, being trusted. Gavin no longer had time for himself or his passions—not that he had many, but that didn't mean he couldn't complain.

And then Adelaide had come to the estate.

He would say her coming here was like the sun breaking through the clouds after months of rain and dreary skies, but that was too poetic. Adelaide's arrival was largely insignificant. Yet it had changed him. When he'd overheard her singing, Gavin had been overwhelmed by the idea of a dream he'd forgotten. For the first time, he felt like he could breathe again.

He craved that feeling of freedom. Gavin wanted to know how he could achieve that, and as the only variable that had changed in his life recently, he believed Adelaide could help him.

He only needed to get to know her. And what better opportunity than the present?

Besides, Gavin tried to convince himself, he could ask her more about Mistress Scrabs and see if it aligned with what he knew of Lady Alyton.

Grabbing his cloak on his way to the door, Gavin felt weightless. When was the last time he'd taken a stroll through his mother's gardens?

He shook his head. It seemed the opportunity hadn't presented itself to him in a long time. Perhaps it would do him some good.

Swiftly making his way through the estate, Gavin skillfully avoided hallways and passages where servants were going about their tasks or where knights were patrolling. The last thing he wanted was for someone to match his stride and derail him with an urgent conversation that, in all honesty, was rarely of any great importance. Gavin was almost tempted to use his magic and conceal himself, but refrained from doing so. After all, why should he feel the need to in his own home?

By the time he made his way outside, Gavin was breathless. The crisp air filled his lungs. The welcome scent of pine and fresh earth tickled his nostrils. He suspected more rain on the horizon, but paid no mind to the dampness in the air. The fur of his cloak kept the worst of it from settling into his bones. Surveying the garden from the second-story veranda, he searched for Adelaide.

Just as his heart was about to sink, he found her sitting in a patch of sunlight near the burbairé grove. He strode down the stairs with purpose. If anyone had seen him, they'd probably assume Gavin was setting off on some urgent quest. He wasn't entirely convinced that he wasn't.

He was going to ask about Mistress Scrabs. He and Adelaide should talk more about their plan to make the pretense of their relationship more believable.

Wasn't that it?

Gavin swallowed, grateful for the evergreens and roubud blooms. The mixed scent of the winter plants grounded him. They calmed his mind and the warring thoughts racing through his head. Their sweet and savory fragrance eased the guilt looming in the back of his mind. He really had more important things he had to do. His health was important too, and Gavin knew it was only a matter of time before he overextended himself.

One afternoon wouldn't harm him. In fact it was quite the opposite. This was exactly the sort of thing Thomas nagged him about.

Slowing his pace as the first of the burbairés came into view, Gavin's stomach twisted. What if Adelaide didn't want his company? His mind began to examine their interaction earlier, and whether or not she was truly comfortable with her new arrangements and their resulting deception.

Gavin's lips slipped into a frown. He shook the concern from his mind and tried to fix his features. He didn't want Adelaide to think something was wrong, or that he didn't want to be here but was only doing so for the sake of their ruse.

Finally entering the copse of dwarf trees bearing the bittersweet fruit, Gavin couldn't help but grin. The soft rays of the late afternoon sun crowned Adelaide. She was like a statue. If she heard his approach, she didn't acknowledge him. Gavin suspected she was lost in her own mind, ensnared by whatever it distracted her with.

In an attempt not to startle her, he called, "May I join you?"

Adelaide turned to look at him, beginning to stand from the bench. Her lips pulled into a small smile. "Of course."

Her trembling hands rubbed her arms. Gavin instantly went to unclasp his cloak and offer it to her. "Here, take my cloak."

"Won't you be cold?" Adelaide raised her brow. Shaking her head, she countered, "Let's share it."

Gavin froze. "Share it?"

"Yes," Adelaide blinked, "the bench is small enough. We'll just have to stay close to each other." She shifted on her feet. "I mean, if you don't mind?"

"Not at all." Gavin undid the clasp of his cloak and drew closer to Adelaide. Draping one half over her shoulder, he carefully slipped his arm from her side of the cloak as she settled it around herself. "Better?"

Adelaide hummed. "Much better, thank you."

Carefully so as not to disturb the cloak, they sat on the bench.

Adelaide scooted closer to him, her shoulder firmly pressed against his side.

"If you were cold, how come you didn't come back in?" he asked.

Adelaide didn't answer straight away. "I thought the cold would help."

Confusion drew his brows together. "Help with what?"

"It's nothing," Adelaide sighed. "I just didn't want to be inside. I…can't stop thinking about…"

Gavin waited a beat before he replied. "I'll never let it happen again. Whatever you need, just ask. Your safety is important, especially as we draw closer to discovering who Mistress Scrabs is."

He didn't have the courage to add that her safety was of personal interest to him. They hadn't known each other long enough for that to be a rational thought, and yet…it was true.

He stiffened as Adelaide rested her head against his shoulder. "I'm still so tired. How long did you let me sleep for?"

"Not long," he lied, slipping his arm around her. In truth, Adelaide had managed to nap for a couple of hours. He envied her, though not her circumstances. It was no surprise that Adelaide was still fighting the effects of the *statique trosher*. "Have you had anything to eat? I'm afraid you missed lunch."

"I'll eat later."

Gavin closed his eyes. "I really think you should eat something sooner. It'll help with the fatigue."

"I'm flattered by your concern," she mumbled.

Gavin studied her as best as he could given their current position. His eyes lingered over her small smirk. She was teasing him.

Rather than letting her rile him, he continued his genuine inquiries. "If you could have any meal right now, what would it be?"

Slowly, Adelaide sat up and met his gaze. "Any meal?"

Gavin nodded.

"Hm…that's a hard question to answer. I would love to have my mother's thistlesquash stew, but she hasn't made it in years." Adelaide paused, glancing away. "I suppose just something warm. Maybe homak and creamed thistlesquash? Oh, and some kind of bread, of course."

"Of course," he said lightly. "I'll ask Ned to prepare it for dinner."

"Oh, that's not…" Adelaide trailed off. "It's like you're really trying to act like we're together." Gavin's heart panicked, thrumming in his throat. "It's oddly sweet."

"I just want you to feel comfortable. I know what it's like to miss home, and have people to care for. But that was my choice. I can't imagine what your life has been like."

"It hasn't all been bad," she whispered. "And I hope it won't be like this forever."

"I think we can make sure of that."

Adelaide smiled softly. "I hope so."

Chapter Seventeen

Adelaide

For several days after their garden escapade, Adelaide wandered Castle Belmont's estate freely and found ways to occupy her time until Gavin joined her in the late afternoon or early evening. Some days, they even ate breakfast together in the sitting room between the archduke's and archduchess's suites.

At first, Adelaide had admittedly been perturbed by the fact that she couldn't get to her room without first going through Gavin's. But Gavin had been true to his word. He hadn't stepped foot in the archduchess's suite. Sometimes, he'd knocked on her door and leaned against the frame as he spoke to her, making sure she was all right and that she had everything she needed.

An easy smile graced her face. Adelaide watched the frostbitten earth pass underfoot as she wandered through the gardens. She was glad to have met someone like Gavin. Slowly but surely, the worry that constantly simmered in her gut had eased. Almost every night, they talked a little about the Den of Thieves and how Gavin intended to bring Mistress Scrabs, whoever she truly was, before the king with the charge of treason.

But with that came a different flavor of fear: what would Gavin do when he learned she'd been the recipient of the smuggled antibiotic from Darshovi that her mother needed? Would she be tried with treason for her part in the smuggling operation Mistress Scrabs had organized? Adelaide's mood soured. Perhaps she'd only be tried for being in possession of illegal goods and spend a few years in prison or pay a fine she couldn't afford. The soft fur-lined cloak Gavin had lent her turned scratchy. It was better than death, she supposed.

Despite how close they'd gotten since she'd moved into the archduchess's suite and their ruse began, Adelaide couldn't say for certain whether or not Gavin would grant her leniency for her treason.

She had no defense for it either. She could've refused Mistress Scrabs's offer and asked for monetary compensation, but she'd chosen not to. She willingly accepted the medication as payment of her own free will. That, and her love for her mother.

Of course, now she knew it was merely another way for Mistress Scrabs to control her.

Adelaide had no doubt that Gavin would understand that motive, but would he be able to overlook his loyalty to Kordouva and his role in protecting its sovereignty?

She couldn't say.

All Adelaide knew for certain was the next shipment was due in two days' time. She *had* to be there. Somehow, some way, she needed to leave Castle Belmont without garnering any suspicion.

Adelaide swallowed. She was certain that if she told Gavin she needed to visit her family, he wouldn't suspect her of any wrongdoing. As it was, he might not even notice. His days had become fuller the closer the eclipse drew. But it also meant that the estate was teeming with knights from all across Kordouva as they prepared for an attack that might not—that hopefully would not—come.

Or she could say she needed to check in with one of Mistress Scrabs's informants to prevent any mistrust from growing there if he asked.

Adelaide bit her lip. In either case, Gavin might insist on taking an escort with her. He'd already offered to have someone accompany her when she wished to visit her family, so surely he'd offer the same if she were to tell him she intended on reporting to Mistress Scrabs.

Shaking her head, Adelaide drew her new cloak tighter around herself. Her eyes turned toward her surroundings. The evergreens on either side of the path, interspersed with forget-me-nots and roubuds, glistened in the waning sunlight.

Slowly, Adelaide wove her way back. She expected Gavin would be just about finished with his ever-growing pile of paperwork or already looking for her. She decided to check his office first before returning to her room to deposit her cloak there.

She found his office empty. Frowning to herself, Adelaide wondered if she'd find Gavin on her way to the archduchess's suite. It would be funny if they were both looking for each other.

But their paths didn't cross. Sighing heavily as she draped her cloak over the chest at the foot of her bed, Adelaide flopped down on the bed.

As she wondered where Gavin was and if their unstated dinner plans had changed, her eyes wandered over the rich furnishings of the room. Finely woven tapestries hung on the walls, covering nearly every inch of the plastered walls. Those and the enchanted fire that danced eternally in the fireplace kept the harsh winter chill at bay.

While the furnishings were finely made, Adelaide realized the room was rather plain. There wasn't a personal touch to be found on the redwood dresser or the dust-coated vase on her nightstand.

Gavin had explained that the room hadn't been used since his parents moved to the coast and left Castle Belmont entirely to him.

In passing, Adelaide had heard the staff mention that it was nice to see the room used, though no one had spoken to her since she'd moved out of the servant's quarters. Or at least, they hadn't spoken to her like they had before. They were polite and kind, but she worried they were treating her like she was above them. She'd have to put a stop to that, somehow.

More and more she wondered why Gavin had moved her into this room. Was it truly for their ruse? Or had he merely wanted to keep her close so he could observe her? Her frown deepened. She *wanted* to trust Gavin. To some extent, she *did* trust the archduke. Wasn't that the reason why she'd divulged her secret to begin with?

Groaning, Adelaide pressed the palm of her hands to her eyes. She took a deep breath and then another.

She wished her life wasn't so complicated.

If it hadn't been for the severillik, Adelaide wouldn't be here right now. She never would've been manipulated into serving Mistress Scrabs, and she wouldn't be questioning her own heart or the intentions of the White Hawk of Kordouva either.

Her heart sank the more her mind turned over the events since she'd come to Castle Belmont. From the moment she'd arrived, nothing had gone as she'd expected it to. This was supposed to be no different than the others. Archduke Gavin Hughes wasn't supposed to notice her. Adelaide wasn't supposed to trust him. And they certainly weren't supposed to grow closer, like friends might.

"Are you all right?"

Adelaide dragged her hands away from her eyes and glanced toward the door. Gavin stood in the empty doorway, his face pinched with worry.

"Fine," Adelaide said as she dragged herself into a sitting position. "You can come in if you'd like."

Gavin shifted on his feet as if he was inclined to step away and return to his own room before he finally stepped over the threshold. Adelaide watched as he crossed the room, and she patted the bed beside her. The bed dipped as he sat. Their shoulders brushed each other. The contact sent a flurry of emotion through Adelaide. Part comfort and part unease, her mind settled as the scent of Gavin's soap floated over her.

"Are you getting a headache? Or were you troubled?" he asked, studying her intently.

Adelaide shook her head. "No, I was just thinking."

"Would you like to talk about it? I find it helps." He offered her a smile that didn't reach his eyes. Instead, those striking crystal eyes that stole her breath and froze her blood shone with hesitation.

"I was just reflecting on things," Adelaide said slowly. She watched Gavin closely to gauge his reaction and found a focused gaze and an unchanged face that might as well have been carved from stone. Her hands settled in her lap. Adelaide assumed that the archduke's undivided attention was encouragement enough to continue. She tried to organize her thoughts and gather her courage. Taking a breath, she quickly added, "Sometimes I wonder what my life would be like if I hadn't become a pickpocket." She hoped Gavin hadn't heard her hurried admission.

But it lightened her heart to free the words from the depths of her mind, her soul.

Gavin's hand grazed hers. Adelaide glanced down at the warm touch and back at Gavin. His eyes had turned molten, his lips turned down in a sympathetic frown. Hesitantly, Adelaide let Gavin lace their fingers together, pulling her hands away from their anxious union. Her chest buzzed anxiously in spite of the comfort his touch offered her.

"If it's any consolation," he replied, his voice low, "I don't think there are many people who wouldn't do something similar for someone they love."

"Do you think?"

"I do," he said confidently, "and sometimes they do so without remorse for their actions. You're kind, Adelaide. I think you're much too harsh when it comes to yourself."

Adelaide's heart stirred. Her eyes flicked to his lips before she caught herself and she glanced away. She couldn't allow herself to get swept away by kind words and focused attention. Frowning at the voice chastising her, Adelaide meant to pull away, but never got the chance to.

Gavin must have mistaken her reaction for disbelief because he quickly added, "I mean it, truly." The bed groaned as he stood swiftly and kneeled in front of her. He clasped her hands firmly in one of his. The other cupped her cheek like a silent plea for her to look at him.

The gesture coaxed Adelaide into looking up. When she did, she found their faces were just inches apart. Adelaide tried to keep her breathing steady, but still she could feel the fluttering in her throat as her heart beat faster and faster. She didn't dare let her gaze drop to his lips again. Even so, Adelaide could still see the soft smile he offered as he stared up at her. Slowly, Gavin's thumb brushed over her cheek. Adelaide longed to lean into his warm touch. Her heart ached.

"Tell me if you don't want me to kiss you," he said slowly, his voice barely a murmur.

Adelaide swallowed thickly. That was all she wanted. She wanted him to kiss her, and to hold her, and to tell her the loving look in his eyes was real and that the closeness they'd achieved wasn't a manifestation of their plan. She wanted him to sweep her off her feet and help her start over, and to forgive her for her past.

Her heart and her body ached for the warm affection glowing in his eyes, melting her soul and all the threats hanging over her before they managed to detain her feelings.

Adelaide took a deep, almost ragged breath. Her mind fumbled to find a resolve she didn't want to feel. All she wanted was for this moment to last. She ached for it to lead to something wonderful and true, something safe and sure, something that could be love.

Instead, Adelaide forced herself to turn her head away. "You shouldn't kiss me," she whispered. Her eyes fell shut against the sting of tears.

Just once, Adelaide wanted to listen to her heart.

But she couldn't.

Goosebumps erupted along her arms as Gavin pulled away. Adelaide loathed the shadow lingering over her heart as Gavin's footsteps indicated the growing distance between them, as he stepped away.

"I know you're hiding things from me, and that you feel you can't trust me," Gavin started, "but I wish you would choose your own happiness, even if it doesn't include me. But believe me when I say I hope it means choosing me too."

The floor creaked. Adelaide's eyes flew open. Whipping her head up, her heart spasmed. Her tongue burned. She wished she could retract her words, to tell him exactly why he shouldn't want to kiss her, even though that was all she wanted. Gavin's back was already to her, and he'd begun his retreat to his room.

A shock of electricity burst through her. Before Adelaide could stop herself, she lunged across the room and grabbed a handful of his shirt.

"Please," she said breathlessly as she rested her forehead on his back, not even fully understanding what it was she was begging for in that exact heartbeat. She breathed deeply and savored the warmth that radiated from him if only for a moment.

Adelaide's heartbeat echoed in her ears ominously as she felt him stiffen against her fingers. Her grip faltered. Slowly, he turned back around to look at her. His face was unreadable, void of any emotion known to her. Gavin caught her wrist as her fingers slipped from his shirt in her disappointment.

This was it. He was leaving. Gavin wouldn't be her beacon, her safeguard.

Before she could even blink or the first of her tears could fall, Gavin had drawn her close to him and wrapped his arms around her, enveloping Adelaide in that warmth she'd come to crave.

His chest vibrated against her forehead as she buried her face in his embrace, too afraid and uncertain to meet his eyes.

"Let me make one thing clear, Adelaide," he said softly. His voice held no threat, no hint of danger, not even the slightest of edges. Instead, it was smooth and gentle even as the words themselves cut deep into her marrow. The gravelly tone made her shiver. "I won't be discarded, by anyone. You don't have to tell me everything, or anything at all, but if you want me, it can't be when it's convenient for you. I don't do halfway. So if you want to do this, to be together no matter how many steps we have to take to meet in the middle, just know I'll be here. I really want us to be together, for this not to be some ruse or part of an investigation. Just know that."

Adelaide curled her fingers against his chest, breathing in the scent of his soap and the wind.

"There's…there's something I need to tell you, Gavin."

He held her tighter. "Whatever it is, it won't change my mind."

Adelaide hoped he was right. Taking a deep breath, she explained, "Do you remember that day, after…" She swallowed, finding it hard to speak about it. Adelaide didn't like to dwell on events such as that one. It clouded her mind and prevented her from living what she could of her life as her own. Moments like that hung over her soul, waiting to snatch it up and consume her. She tried again, forcing the words past her teeth. "After Mistress Scrabs had…punished me for what happened to Jeffery—"

"*That's* why she used *statique trosher* on you?" he growled.

Adelaide flushed. "Yes. That and I was late in reporting my progress to her. But that's not why I brought this up. It's not important—"

"It is to me," he interrupted. "She hurt you."

"I'm fine," Adelaide assured him, finally drawing her eyes to meet his. When she did, she found that behind the concern and the way his care for her glowed so brightly in his blue eyes was a fire that would undoubtedly protect all Gavin cared for—including her. She shivered under the intensity of his gaze. Adelaide's lips pulled into a whisper of a smile. Her heart flooded with a dazzling warmth. "You made certain of that."

Gavin hummed, staring back at her. He gently tucked a strand of her hair behind her ear and cupped her face with his callused hand, lightly stroking her cheek with his thumb.

Adelaide leaned into the touch, savoring his gentleness. Whether he knew it or not, Gavin had made it very hard for her to distance her heart from him. Standing here, with him, like this, Adelaide found she cared less and less about reality or where these feelings would bring her.

"She ordered me to steal your heart, Gavin," Adelaide murmured at last. "She wanted me to distract you so that the Eye of Behelwer would be easier to steal."

Gavin smirked. "Well then, you've succeeded in one area. My heart is yours."

Adelaide opened and closed her mouth. Her stomach twisted, knotting itself up in a panic.

"I didn't know it, but I think from the moment we met, my heart was yours. I kept telling myself it was merely interest because I suspected you of being a thief, but the more I watched you and our paths crossed, the more I realized I was seeking you out. I wanted to get to know you. And then I overheard you singing, and I finally understood what my heart already knew." Adelaide tried to turn away, to hide her embarrassment, but Gavin caught her chin and tilted her face up. "It was inevitable, Adelaide. You're a puzzle to me, and I want to learn about every piece of you."

Adelaide's gaze drifted to his lips. The words ordering him to kiss her were on the tip of her tongue, but she swallowed them down.

Adelaide dragged her eyes away from his lips. When her eyes met his, Adelaide's breath caught in her throat at the storm of emotion marring Gavin's crystal blue eyes. Staring back into the heart of that stormy sea, Adelaide tentatively reached her hand up to his face. Lightly tracing her fingertips across the planes of his cheekbones and down to his jaw, Adelaide's resolve weakened.

"I think you should kiss me," she murmured.

Gavin smiled. "I'd love nothing more."

Adelaide melted at the press of his lips against hers. Her knees went weak. Gavin's kiss was soft but deep and thorough. Her fingers dug into his shoulders and found the firm muscles there. Fearful that her legs would collapse beneath her, Adelaide was grateful for Gavin's arms around her. She clung to him as eagerly as he brought her closer to him. Her lungs burned, and she couldn't ignore the ache any longer. Reluctantly, she pulled away.

"Stay," she breathed. "Please."

Chapter Eighteen

Gavin

Gavin held Adelaide gently. Terrified of moving, he could only lay there. Eventually, Gavin found himself grateful for the chance to study her unencumbered by fear or the mask she wore in her waking moments. She was at peace in her sleep.

That, and this was the first time since Penumbra's War had ended that he'd allowed himself to linger in bed. Despite the warmth radiating off of Adelaide curled up against him, and the soft light of the sun poking through the cracks in the shutters drawn over the windows of the archduchess's suite, Gavin's mind couldn't wholly stop.

He replayed the almost desperate way he'd kissed Adelaide last night. The moment their lips met was like a spark. It flitted through him, through his blood, and straight into his core. Gavin hadn't wanted to let go. It didn't even matter that he'd needed to breathe. All he'd cared about was her lips on his and how close he could possibly hold her, to know she was real and that this moment wasn't a cruel dream he'd eventually wake from.

Absently, Gavin rubbed his hand up and down her back. He studied her, drinking in the peace on her face and the freedom of her sleep-marred features. Her hair splayed across the bed behind her. He stared at the soft curl in the tips of her hair, lost once more in the memory of her lips against his and the way she'd placed his hands on her waist, allowing him to wander.

He hoped she didn't regret last night.

At the thought, Gavin's rhythm faltered until he'd nearly stopped rubbing her back.

Adelaide sighed softly and shifted in her sleep. As she burrowed herself deeper into the blankets, her hands curled against his shirt. Gavin stiffened, worried he'd woken her.

When she tilted her face up, Adelaide's arm tightened around his waist. She smiled slowly. The softness of sleep still graced her features. It was the most at ease Gavin had ever seen her.

"You're still here," she breathed.

"Where else would I be?" he asked, stroking her hair.

She snuggled closer to him and shrugged. "Your office, like you are every morning."

"Except for the days we have breakfast together."

"You come back on those days to eat with me," Adelaide laughed.

"And how would you know that?"

"Sometimes I hear you leave your room. Sometimes I hear you come back."

"And what about today?" he found himself asking.

Adelaide frowned, looking up at him. "What about it?"

"Do you…" How was he supposed to phrase this? "Do you like that I'm still here?"

Slowly, Adelaide pulled herself up so that they were face to face. She cupped his face, and Gavin found himself leaning into the touch. He gently wrapped his fingers around her wrist, content for a heartbeat to simply exist in this moment. All he knew was that: contentedness.

From the moment her expressive emerald eyes had turned on him, all his worries had melted away like the winter frost.

"I very much like that you're still here," she said softly. Before her words had even sunk into his mind, Adelaide pressed a kiss to his forehead. He leaned forward as she pulled away in the hopes that a proper kiss might be shared. Gavin had to keep himself from groaning as it became apparent their lips weren't to meet this morning. "I hope…I hope this isn't the last…"

Gavin grabbed her hand. "It won't be."

Adelaide's smile didn't reach her eyes.

"Adelaide," he continued, stroking his thumb across her knuckles, "I have no intentions of ever hurting you, or using you. You know that, right?"

"I want to believe you…it's just that…" She took a deep breath. "You're an archduke, Gavin. We're supposed to be…this was a ruse, and yet it feels real."

"It *is* real. I'm here, and I won't be going anywhere anytime soon," he assured her. "You're not someone to be forgotten easily, Adelaide."

She laughed, a broken sound that cleaved his heart in two. "I am, though. I've survived these last four years only because I'm no one remarkable. You're supposed to forget me."

"Am I?" he said. Fire licked at his veins. Was that what Adelaide truly believed? That she was someone to be overlooked? "And, pray tell, why 'should' I?"

"I don't know," she whispered, letting her eyes fall shut. "I'm sorry."

"For what? Not trusting an archduke? Being concerned?" Gavin brushed her hair back from her face, tracing the shell of her ear. Adelaide shivered under his touch, and Gavin wanted nothing more than to kiss her right then and there or pull her into his lap to be closer together. Instead, Gavin tamped the desire down and settled his hand on her waist. "I'm happy you asked me. I feel better knowing that you're thinking about this seriously, and not playing a part in a scheme, mine or Mistress Scrabs's."

Adelaide blinked. Staring at him wide-eyed and slack-jawed, she asked, "Really?"

"I don't want to take advantage of you," he explained. "I was worried you'd wake up and regret trusting me."

The corners of Adelaide's lips turned up. "I was only worried because you looked pained when I first woke up. I thought you regretted last night."

Gavin blinked. Not for a moment had he felt conflicted in his feelings for Adelaide, especially not when he'd come into her room last night. "Never. It seems you and I had the same worry."

Adelaide rested her head against his shoulder. "We can't stay like this today."

"Are you telling me or trying to convince yourself?" he teased.

"Both," she mumbled. She sat up again, and this time, the tension had settled over her, and Gavin could almost see the dark clouds that hovered over her.

He would not put Adelaide in danger. He'd promised.

Sighing, Gavin's shoulders slumped. He longed to stay too, but knew the longer he did, the worse Darshovi's threat grew as the eclipse was only ten days away. Reluctantly, Gavin pulled away from Adelaide and forced himself to sit up. "I'll make sure to be done in time for dinner."

"That's fine." Adelaide sat up and pulled the blankets around herself. Gavin raised his brow at the withdrawn look that blanketed her features. "I was thinking it's about time I report to an informant of Mistress Scrabs's today before something bad happens again."

Gavin froze. It would have been better had he not gotten up at all. Then neither of them would have to go about their day, and reality wouldn't be crashing in around them now.

"You know I have to," she said, her eyes wide and pleading.

Gavin nodded. He did. Rationally, he knew Adelaide was right and that keeping her routine would keep her safe, but his mind couldn't help but see the way her face had tensed with pain every time she moved or how long she'd slept after her last encounter with Mistress Scrabs.

"Do you have to go alone?" he finally asked. He tried not to clench his teeth. He didn't want her to go at all.

"It would be helpful, yes."

"Someone will follow you then," Gavin said, "and if it comes into question, it will only look like I suspect you of something."

"At best," Adelaide argued. "Gavin, please. I have to go alone. Besides, Mistress Scrabs has no reason to be there today. This is just a routine touchstone so she doesn't get suspicious of me. I'll be fine."

Gavin studied her. Her hands twisted the blankets in her fists. She stared at him with what could only be desperation. Was there something she wasn't telling him?

"All right," he relented. "I guess it makes sense. You should go about your usual routine. That's probably the best way to keep you safe."

"My thoughts exactly."

Running a hand through his hair, he left the bed and crossed the room. Lost in thought, Gavin hadn't heard Adelaide get up and follow in his path across the room. Gasping as her arms wrapped around him from behind, he turned.

"Adelaide?"

"I don't know," she mumbled. "I just…I didn't want to leave things so awkwardly between us. It could only be my insecurity, but I have a bad feeling about today."

"Then don't go," he pleaded, wrapping her in his embrace.

"I have to."

"Then take someone with you."

"I can't."

"Then promise me you'll be safe," he said, running his thumb lightly across her bottom lip.

"I promise," she whispered. Standing on the tips of her toes, Adelaide pressed her lips to his. Gavin closed his eyes and wrapped his arms around her to pull her closer. Nearly sighing, Gavin tilted his head to deepen the kiss, just wanting this moment to last.

Adelaide's lips were soft and gone too soon. As she pulled away, it left him feeling empty as her warmth was replaced by the cool air of the archduchess's suite. "I'll be safe."

"Thank you," he breathed. Kissing the top of her head, Gavin added, "If anything were to happen to you, I'd never forgive myself."

Chapter Nineteen

Adelaide

Adelaide wrapped her arms around herself. Dazed by the recent events, she watched with a burdened heart as Gavin slipped from the room. Would it have been too much to stay in each other's arms for a moment longer?

Or would the world have collapsed around them?

Adelaide sighed. She didn't have the time to linger on idle fantasies, not when she'd willingly offered herself up as a sacrificial agent for his and Sir Maxwell's investigation. Even if she hadn't told Gavin of her connection to Mistress Scrabs, she'd still have to report her progress to the Den of Thieves. The only benefit was that she didn't have to sneak about. In truth, her confession had only made this task harder for her. Gavin was much too worried about her—even though she didn't mind his concern. In fact, she found it quite endearing. After so long, it was nice to have someone to confide in, who checked on her, whom she could depend on if needed.

But trusting Gavin had complicated things.

All Adelaide could truly do in this moment, aside from preparing for the day ahead, was hope against all odds that Gavin wouldn't send someone to watch over her and catch her in the act of treason.

Adelaide slipped out of her nightshirt with a shiver. She wondered what would happen if Gavin ever found out that she was involved with smuggling the Darshovian medicine her mother and countless others so desperately needed into Kordouva. Would he care enough to save her from the gallows? Would helping him stop the Master of Thieves be enough to earn her a lesser sentence?

Adelaide chewed her bottom lip. She hoped she would never find out.

Adelaide's eyes flitted over every nook and cranny of the crooked buildings as she glanced up and down the street. She anxiously searched the shadows for any lingering forms, but found none. Breathing a sigh of relief, she crossed the street and tried the handle of the Hawk & Thorne Inn. Finding it locked, Adelaide cursed under her breath. Sliding a pin from her hair, she cast a glance about to ensure no one was observing her. With not a soul to be found, Adelaide bent the pin accordingly and set it into the lock. Patiently feeling the shift of the tumblers, Adelaide worked at the lock. She sighed when it finally clicked and let herself inside.

"Dylan, it's me," she called, closing the door behind her.

Dusty light filled the tavern. Adelaide cautiously took a step farther into the room, peering through the dim light that battled against the thin curtains pulled over the windows.

Where was Dylan?

Gripping the warm hilt of the dagger Ethan had given her, Adelaide examined the empty room. It could've been her imagination, but the thick tension in the inn made goosebumps erupt along her arms.

At this time of day, people should've been milling around. Someone should have been here—Dylan should've been here.

The only other time Adelaide had ever seen the inn closed and shuttered against the world was the day Mistress Scrabs had come to punish her for Jeffery's capture.

Careful not to make a sound, Adelaide pulled her dagger from its sheath and edged her way toward the bar. Her gaze flitted about the room, knowing she could trust nothing.

With a long look toward the barren tavern, Adelaide twisted the handle of the door behind the bar. The *squeak* of the hinges pierced the room like a cannon blast. Adelaide's heart pounded between her ears. Nothing followed in the wake of the disturbance. She strained her ears. The stale air of the inn's storeroom wafted up the stairs and assaulted her nose. Low voices could be heard from down below. Adelaide pressed her lips together.

Could it be Dylan was only taking inventory?

Forcing herself to descend the worn staircase, Adelaide clutched her dagger closer to her chest. The hilt radiated heat. By the time she'd reached the bottom of the stairs, Adelaide had begun to wish she'd stayed at Castle Belmont, or had gone straight to the docks to inquire about the medicine directly with Mistress Scrabs's privateer. But it was too late to turn back now.

Adelaide did her best to tamp down the chill that crawled down her spine. The voices became more distinguishable with each step she took. She stuck to the shadows between the bouncing light cast by the flickering lanterns, hiding behind crates and barrels scattered throughout the cellar and along the walls.

As she came to the end of the stored goods, Adelaide peeked around the corner of the crate. Her eyes landed on her worst fear, and her throat closed.

Mistress Scrabs, and a man she didn't recognize.

"It shouldn't be much longer now," Mistress Scrabs said airily. She sat delicately atop a barrel across the way, watching as the man clothed in a dark cloak paced before her. He had his hands clasped behind his back and made stiff, quick turns as he paced. Agitation rolled off of him in waves. Though he was slight, he seemed to dominate the space. Shadows seemed to cling to him. Adelaide forced herself to swallow. She shouldn't be here.

Mistress Scrabs continued, "My source within Castle Belmont says the two have grown fond of each other. They even spent the night together."

"I don't see how that would help us," the man spat. "We cannot wait for the eclipse."

"I know this." Mistress Scrabs slipped from the barrel and walked right up to the man. Putting her hands on his chest to stop his pacing, Mistress Scrabs smiled sharply under her mask. "That's why we're going to steal the Eye of Behelwer and use it to force the eclipse sooner and bolster your magic to keep opening portals into Penumbra."

Adelaide nearly stumbled. Had she heard that correctly? Could the Eye be used to move celestial bodies? Could they really make the eclipse happen sooner than the astronomers anticipated it would?

For all their sakes, she hoped not. She fought against a shudder as old memories of Penumbra's War flitted through her mind. Not nearly enough time had passed between now and then. Seven years had hardly healed Kordouva.

"And you're going to steal it for us, isn't that right, Adelaide?"

Adelaide's blood froze. Her mouth went dry.

"Come now, Addie," Mistress Scrabs taunted her as she turned on her heel and stared directly at Adelaide's hiding place. "I know you're there. Don't make me come and get you. It will only be harder for you if I do."

Adelaide couldn't catch her breath. She swallowed hard and sheathed her dagger. Stiff with fear, she forced herself to stand, ensuring that her cloak hid the weapon, and joined the pair in the weak glow of the lantern. Her mind whirred. She needed to say something, anything, that might save herself.

"I'm sorry," she stammered. "I didn't mean to intrude. I was only looking for Dylan."

Mistress Scrabs tilted her head. A mocking frown settled over her lips. "Oh? You haven't heard?"

Dread twisted in Adelaide's gut. She shook her head.

"Poor dear," Mistress Scrabs said, approaching her. Standing face-to-face with her, Mistress Scrabs put a hand on Adelaide's shoulder like someone offering comfort might. It only made the buzzing in

Adelaide's chest crescendo. She waited for the pain to flood her system. But none came. Instead, Mistress Scrabs frowned and squeezed her shoulder a fraction too hard.

"I hate to be the one to tell you this, Addie, but Dylan's dead. Caught spying on us, I'm afraid."

"That's horrible," Adelaide said numbly. Her mind seized. Any and all thought came to a harsh stop. Adelaide could feel her chest heaving, but her conscious mind was so far removed from any sense, she felt nothing at all.

"I knew you would be sympathetic." Mistress Scrabs smiled. Her grip on Adelaide's shoulder eased. "If only everyone could be as understanding."

The man scoffed. "Are you quite done yet?"

Mistress Scrabs blissfully pulled away from her, but not before Adelaide had seen the twitch in her jaw and the roll of her eyes. Adelaide shifted on her feet. She'd have to remember that for later. She didn't know if the tension between them would be helpful, but surely it could help drive them apart if only she knew how or what their goals were.

"I find it rude that someone who has very little to contribute to our efforts has such an outspoken impatience," The Master of Thieves replied evenly. Adelaide wanted to run, knowing that tone was a precursor to something awful. "Adelaide is an excellent thief, perfectly unremarkable, reliable, and unassuming."

Adelaide's hand gravitated toward her wrist and began to rub it soothingly, as if she could make herself small enough to disappear. The action offered her little comfort. Until she was dismissed, there was nothing she could do but stand there obediently and listen as Mistress Scrabs whittled away at her self-worth, all under the guise of praising her usefulness.

The man let out a long-suffering sigh. Adelaide observed him through her lashes, too ashamed and frightened to look at him directly.

"I don't know how I ever let you convince me of your plan, My Lady."

"I wouldn't be me without my charms, now would I, Your Highness?" Mistress Scrabs purred. The edge in her voice dulled. She smoothed a hand up the man's chest and wrapped her hand around the back of his neck, pressing herself up against him.

Nausea burned in Adelaide's gut. Highness?

All discretion fled. Adelaide outwardly studied the man, his dark hair and deep-set eyes. His *golden* eyes.

Darshovi.

A Darshovian royal.

Adelaide's head pounded. Faintness filled her bones. Her mind spun, struggling to comprehend just who she was looking at—and the relationship implied between him and the Master of Thieves.

It should have been impossible. She was seeing a ghost, an illusion, a trick.

Yet a tiny voice tried to convince her that maybe she wasn't.

Darshovi's fifth prince, Prince Branigan, was rumored to be the only survivor of the country's royal family in the wake of Penumbra's War, but up until this very moment, Adelaide hadn't believed the speculation to be more than idle gossip.

But if she was right, and the golden eyes of the man before her weren't an illusion, the hallmark of the Darshovi's royal family had given her all she needed to know.

The King of Kordouva had been right to seek out the Eye of Behelwer and hide it. Gavin had been right to ruthlessly search for Mistress Scrabs and reveal her.

The prince's gaze slid to her over Mistress Scrabs's shoulder. Adelaide squirmed under the full weight of his calculating gaze. "How can we trust her? What's to say the archduke hasn't gotten in her head?"

An amused smirk pulled at Mistress Scrabs's lips, though her eyes narrowed as she turned to look at Adelaide. "I don't see how the archduke could. Not when I've already gone through the hassle of securing her mother's medicine and my guards *personally* delivered it to Addie's family's home. Isn't that right, Adelaide?"

The unspoken threat rattled her conscience. Adelaide feared she'd be sick. Mistress Scrabs's men were at her home. A clammy sweat broke out along the back of her neck. They had her family. "Right. Thank you, My Lady."

"Then we're agreed." Prince Branigan hummed. The shadows around him seemed to grow thicker, darker. "You'll steal the Eye for us, and if you succeed, you'll be rewarded handsomely. If you fail… Well, I suppose you won't, now, will you? Not if you want to save your family. I hear those who disappoint the Master of Thieves suffer dearly."

"Of course, Your Highness." Adelaide forced herself to speak around the rocks in her throat. "I should return to Castle Belmont before His Grace starts searching for me."

"Were you that successful in stealing his heart, Addie, dear?"

Adelaide nodded weakly. "It's what you asked of me, My Lady."

Mistress Scrabs hummed, apparently pleased with her response. "Wonderful. Then all that's left is for you to deliver the Eye to us and return to Belmont to keep the archduke distracted for us."

Adelaide's head spun. She wanted to faint. She wished the ground would swallow her whole so she wouldn't have to face this situation any longer, or worse: face Gavin now that Mistress Scrabs had forced her hand.

Instead, she bowed her head and offered a quiet affirmation at the order. A silent tear trailed down her cheek as she turned away. Shame licked at her bones as Adelaide receded farther within herself.

She wished it had never come to any of this.

Chapter Twenty

Gavin

Gavin gritted his teeth. He couldn't wait until he and William thought of a better solution to satiate the Eye of Behelwer. Until then, he'd just have to bear the twice-daily hike up to the vault. Dragging a hand through his hair, Gavin mentally prepared himself for the massive draw of energy he was about to encounter as he turned the corner.

"Adelaide?"

At the end of the hall, Adelaide jumped and whirled around to face him. Under any other circumstance, the small squeak she let out would've made him smile. But the fact that she was standing right in front of the magical barrier that stood as the vault's entrance, reaching all about for a trigger that didn't exist had Gavin ensnared by confusion.

"Gavin!" she gasped. "I…This—" Adelaide pressed her hands to her eyes. He watched her closely, waiting patiently for an explanation. He crossed his arms over his chest. Had he fallen for an act after all?

Gavin shook his head. It couldn't be. He knew Adelaide. She did not willfully harbor ill intent toward him or Castle Belmont. So how had it come to this? What had changed?

Gavin waited for the deep breaths to turn into sobs. But they didn't.

Instead, Adelaide withdrew her hands. Playing with her fingers, she said, "I can explain. Please."

"Look at me, Adelaide."

An eternity passed in the time it took for Adelaide to meet his gaze. When she did, Gavin's heart nearly fractured. The mixed emotions swirling in her eyes made him think of the day she'd come into his office after Mistress Scrabs had used *statique trosher* on her.

Fear, desperation, pain, and a sadness that cleaved his heart in two lay bare under his study of her.

"What's happened?" he asked quietly, his tone harsher than he'd intended it to be. Adelaide flinched at the hard edge to his words. Gavin forced himself to take a breath. Reaching out to her slowly, Gavin settled his hands on her shoulders. He rubbed her arms in an attempt to soothe her. "I'm sorry. I didn't mean to be short with you. I only want to know what's happened."

"She threatened my family," Adelaide said hoarsely, like she was holding back tears or couldn't speak. "I have to bring her the Eye."

"We can't give her the Eye," Gavin interrupted.

Adelaide inhaled sharply. "What else can we do? Gavin, my fam—they have my family."

Gavin reached a hand up. When she didn't move away or show any sign to discourage his touch, Gavin gently wiped away her tears. There were too many questions and details to sort through. He didn't know which to ask first. "Who else knows about this threat?"

"Just you," she whispered. "And whoever else Mistress Scrabs has working for her within Castle Belmont."

Gavin's heart spasmed. "Inside Castle Belmont? Aside from you?"

"Yes. I just learned about them today. My contact…he's dead." Adelaide hiccupped, overtaken by a sob. Gavin moved to wrap her in his arms in an effort to offer what little comfort he could.

Adelaide pressed her hands against his chest and shook her head solemnly. "There's something else…something you need to tell the king."

Gavin tilted his head. Dread sank into his bones. "What is it?"

"The Darshovian prince is alive. I saw him with Mistress Scrabs at the inn. *They* want the Eye of Behelwer."

Gavin's mouth went dry. "To do what?"

"They think they can make the eclipse happen sooner by using the Eye. I think they want to attack Kordouva."

"If that's possible…they want to surprise us." Gavin's mind reeled. He didn't doubt Adelaide, but he couldn't make sense of it all.

"Is it?" Adelaide insisted. "Could the Eye of Behelwer really shift the cosmos?"

Gavin considered the question. His stomach tightened. "I don't know. Maybe, given the nature of the prince's powers and connection to the Penumbral Realm, but I couldn't say for certain. The Eye amplifies power. Branigan would have to be the strongest magic user in the world for their plan to work. Or…they could destroy the very fabric of our universe in their attempt."

Adelaide paled, her face drawn with apprehension. Gavin reached for her hand and squeezed. "I won't let that happen."

Her shoulders tensed, but still she nodded. "I know."

"Just as I won't let anything happen to your family."

Adelaide's lips twitched as if she wanted to smile. Sadness swam in her eyes. Gavin stroked his thumb across her cheek. He wished they had time. He craved the time to comfort her but knew they hadn't many heartbeats to spare if they wanted to save her family and stop Mistress Scrabs.

"Do you know what Mistress Scrabs wants more than anything?" Gavin asked.

Adelaide frowned. Her brows drew together in her confusion. "Why does that matter to you now? Shouldn't we—"

"Please," he said, "This could help us."

Adelaide looked at him doubtfully. "I would say power. More than anything, Mistress Scrabs wants power. It's the only thing she could stand to gain by aligning herself with the only surviving heir to the Darshovi throne."

"Because she has plenty of wealth and influence already as the Master of Thieves, but has to hide who she is."

The pieces of the puzzle Gavin had been toiling over clicked into place.

"Status," Adelaide breathed. "Of course! She wants the status her power—"

Adelaide gasped as he picked her up, spinning her around.

Laughing, she asked, "What are you doing?"

"You're amazing, Adelaide," he said, setting her down. Kissing her forehead, he explained, "I know who Mistress Scrabs is. I have to go and speak with William. I'll explain everything later, I promise! Just be ready to meet with Mistress Scrabs in an hour."

"What about my family?" she called after him.

Gavin stopped short. Turning around, he pressed a hand over his heart and bowed. "They'll be safe, I promise."

Chapter Twenty-One

Adelaide

Adelaide stood helplessly where Gavin had left her, staring after him in equal parts desperation and gratefulness. She tried to steady her breathing, willing the panic flitting about her chest to dissipate. The cold walls of the hallway loomed ominously in her peripheral vision. They drew nearer to her and squeezed the breath from her lungs as they closed in around her as she waited.

Her heart pounded against her chest. She was certain it would burst through her skin. Her fingers itched. Adelaide frantically tried to calm herself down as the half-formed desire to do something—*anything*—cartwheeled through her bloodstream.

But the reality was there wasn't any way for her to help her family. She was entirely at the mercy of the newfound trust she'd placed in Gavin and hoped he had a plan to save her family. She didn't even care if they apprehended Mistress Scrabs and the prince. All she wanted was for her family to be safe, and she had to trust Gavin. She couldn't dethorn the stem herself, and that fact made grief and anxiety buzz through her veins. She had no choice but to be pricked or to take care. That was all she could do.

Shaking out her hands, Adelaide meant to find her way downstairs. At the sound of quick footsteps and movement out of the corner of her eye, Adelaide stopped. Sir Maxwell came barreling around the corner. Adelaide's heart thrummed in her throat.

Breathless, he ground to a halt a few feet away from her as their eyes met. Adelaide watched him, hoping he'd come to tell her all that Gavin hadn't. His shoulders heaved with each breath he took, as if he'd rushed here immediately after meeting with Gavin. Had they known she hadn't moved from this spot? Or had he tried searching for her elsewhere first?

Straightening, Sir Maxwell slowly approached her and the wall that guarded all of Gavin's treasures. "Gavin's told me everything. Your family's going to be all right, Adelaide. I promise. We'll get them through this."

"What is Gavin planning?" she asked, though she didn't have much hope of receiving an answer.

Sir Maxwell hesitated, shifting on his feet. "I'm to accompany you to meet with Mistress Scrabs and the Darshovian prince. To protect you and the Eye."

"Wait," Adelaide said. Her brows drew together in confusion. "Are we really going to bring the Eye with us? Isn't that too great of a risk?"

Sir Maxwell brushed past her. In a constant state of motion, he briefly explained how Gavin intended to do just as Mistress Scrabs had ordered Adelaide to do. Raising his hand so his open palm was mere inches from the wall, Sir Maxwell added, "I'm sure nothing bad will happen. We'll make certain of it."

Adelaide stared in wonder as sparks of magic accumulated near Sir Maxwell's hand. Her brows furrowed as the wall began to ripple and at what Sir Maxwell wasn't saying. "What about Gavin? Where will he be?"

Sir Maxwell offered her a self-assured smile. "Gavin intends to gather the forces necessary to ensure your family's safety. Then they will come to us and arrest Mistress Scrabs and Darshovi's sole heir."

"But won't Mistress Scrabs suspect something is amiss if you accompany me?" Fear licked at Adelaide's insides, curling in her blood. None of this sounded like a well-thought-out plan. It didn't even sound like a half-baked idea. It was a flimsy response at best and a failure from the start at worst. Adelaide grabbed Sir Maxwell, stopping him from walking through what she now understood to be a magical barricade. "I'm not sure this is right. Maybe we should stall them as long as we can until Gavin and his forces reach us."

"The Eye will be perfectly safe, I promise." Sir Maxwell patted her hand. His earnestness did nothing to soothe her. "Adelaide…I need you to let me go. Gavin only granted me a limited amount of time to get into the vault, or else he'll have to come up here and get it for us. I promise—everything will be fine. Gavin will protect your family and then come and meet us."

She nodded, letting her hand slip from his arm. The impatience in his eyes made her feel small. She bit her tongue to prevent herself from asking any more questions.

A nameless anchor sank to the pit of Adelaide's stomach as she watched Sir Maxwell disappear into the vault.

Could Gavin and whatever assembly he mustered truly subdue Mistress Scrabs and her newly realized ally?

Adelaide bit her lip. There had to be more to Gavin's plan than Sir Maxwell had explained to her. Giving Mistress Scrabs and the Darshovian prince the Eye of Behelwer simply wasn't an option, but what was Adelaide supposed to do?

Adelaide fidgeted, adjusting the ties of the warm cloak Gavin had given her. It smelled like Castle Belmont—like Gavin. The scent was oddly comforting to her as the carriage jostled and ambled down the city streets. Sir Maxwell had insisted they take it rather than walk, claiming it would be faster. Adelaide worried it was too conspicuous, especially for something as clandestine as their mission felt. But it was no use in convincing Sir Maxwell otherwise.

Try as she might, Adelaide couldn't keep herself from searching through the darkness for hidden allies or a means of escape. She feared her straying eyes would give away both her nerves and their plan. She needed to temper herself before it was time to face Mistress Scrabs and that unnerving myth that was the fifth prince of Darshovi.

If she didn't, they would fail.

"There's no need to be frightened, Adelaide," Sir Maxwell said, breaking the silence at last. "Everything will be just fine."

Adelaide wished she could have Sir Maxwell's confidence—though she was grateful not to have the experience it was likely forged by. "I'm sure you're right," she replied slowly, twisting her hands in her skirt. "I just can't help but be nervous. All I can think about is my family."

Sir Maxwell didn't reply right away. In the pause that ensued, dread unfurled in Adelaide's gut and began to squirm through her veins.

She held her breath, waiting. Anxiety gnawed at the forefront of her mind. Try as she might, Adelaide couldn't banish the shadows that crept forward from the far reaches of her mind with their whispers of danger. Smoothing out the fabric of her skirt, Adelaide sat back in her seat and drew her arms under her cloak. Folding her arms over her chest, Adelaide's elbow knocked into the pommel of her dagger. She jerked away from it, rubbing her elbow.

Why was it so hot to the touch?

Before she could consider any possibility, Sir Maxwell spoke up, stealing her from her puzzlement.

"Every time I find myself walking into danger," he said so quietly Adelaide almost didn't hear it, "I think of my wife. I promise you, Adelaide—I'll do everything I can to ensure your family's safety. Everything I've ever done in my life has been for mine. That's all I think about, every choice I make, every day since I met Evelynn."

Adelaide's heart swelled. "Thank you, Sir Maxwell. That means a lot to me."

Wasn't that all she'd ever done too, think of her family? The nerves in her veins cooled. Adelaide took her first free breath all day.

Chapter Twenty-Two

Gavin

With each bounce of Aves, Gavin's chainmail rattled. The weight of his armor would only grow more burdensome if there was to be a battle tonight. As it was, Gavin was already desperately fighting against his own mind and all the scenarios it had conjured in the wake of Adelaide's news.

Prince Branigan Hunten was a walking nightmare. Since he was able to bend the veil between this reality and the Penumbral Realm—even for a short time—Gavin and his men had to be prepared to face the worst. He couldn't imagine the damage Branigan would be capable of with the Eye of Behelwer. Gavin's worst fear was that the prince would manage to permanently destroy the veil between the realms and finally uphold the bargain the first king of Darshovi had struck with the god Penumbra and its domain a millennia ago.

With any luck, they would find themselves facing only the curiosity of Adelaide's family and the awkwardness of explaining to them the position Adelaide had found herself in. Dueling was one thing, but shattering the fragile lies woven by a loved one was something else entirely. Gavin wasn't certain what he would rather find waiting for him at their farmhouse.

But Adelaide had seemed certain her family was being held captive. She didn't say how she could know, and Gavin hadn't thought to press her. Her urgency was enough—and the Master of Thieves's reputation was formidable enough—Gavin hadn't needed to ask.

Urging his speckled horse down the lane that would finally bring them to Adelaide's home, Gavin's heart thundered between his ears. Still a distance from the house, Gavin wrestled with his mind. He needed a clear head. If he didn't squash the thoughts that ranged from manic screams to creeping whispers, he'd never be able to focus. And if it was truly a battle that awaited him and his men at the house, he wouldn't be of any use to anyone—least of all to Adelaide.

Focusing on his breathing, Gavin looked toward the horizon. Past fields of winter greens and burbairé trees, a quiet calm enveloped Gavin at last. His eyes caught sight of flickering lights up ahead. Candles illuminated the windows of the plain two-story house. A lantern cast a dancing light by the front door. And in the light of the waxing moon was a group of several figures standing out in the field beyond the weathered fence that guarded Adelaide's home.

The moonlight gleamed off their armor.

Gavin glared.

It could only be the fifth prince and whatever forces he commanded.

Gavin held his fist up. Pulling back on the reins, Aves slowed. The thundering hooves behind him faded. Dame Beatrix trotted up beside him.

"What do you think is waiting for us at this house?"

"A battle." Gavin clenched his jaw. "We'll have to see who it is before we make any decisions. If it's the prince, we'll need to dismount. I don't want the horses to get spooked if he opens a gate between the realms."

"Understood, Commander."

Gavin pressed his lips together. He hoped he was wrong.

Gavin hefted his sword and slashed through the shadowy fiemon looming over him. The cool lick of its blade grazed his face, glancing off his skin as the shadow dispersed. Gavin spun and slashed at the creature behind him. His chest heaved. Gavin surveyed the battlefield. His mind spiraled. When would it end?

Gavin's sword flickered. His energy waned, smothered by the

exertion of battle and the ever-present weight of his armor. Sweat beaded between his brow. His face was as hot as the flames engulfing his blade. It was the only way to kill Penumbra's shadows. Despite the battle raging around him and the fiemons bearing down on him, a constant fear plagued his mind: had their plan gone awry? Was Adelaide safe?

At least the Eye of Behelwer was safe within Castle Belmont. There was that small consolation at least.

A shadowy silhouette lumbered toward him. Gavin forced all thoughts from his mind. Staring into the void of the fiemon's gaping mouth, Gavin lifted his sword and cleaved the fiemon in half. The swirling mass of shadow wavered, disappearing into the moonlit night.

All around him, shadows morphed into giant foot soldiers faster than Gavin and his fellow warriors could slay them.

Gritting his teeth, Gavin squared his footing. A fiemon riding a shadowy horse bore down on him. Gavin watched as the warrior raised its spear.

"This is tedious," he grumbled. Jabbing the point of his blade into the ground, Gavin gathered the flames into his hand and manipulated them into a dagger. He raised his arm and threw it.

The rider dissipated into thin air. Without any guidance, the shadow horse reared back on its hind legs and let out a frantic neigh. With little time to waste, Gavin pulled the remaining embers from his cooling sword and stoked them with his magic. His second dagger took care of the horse, sending it back to the Penumbral Realm just as he had done to its rider.

Wiping the sweat from his brow, Gavin surveyed the trampled farmland. The shadows were thick all around. The flickering lights through the darkness were the only indication of where the Belmont knights were fighting foes of their own. Exhaustion weighed heavily upon his shoulders.

The wave of shadow seemed as if it would never stop. Fiemon after fiemon spawned from its swirling depths. Gavin took a deep breath and closed his eyes. Nodding to himself, he reached a hand up to the sky. His magic flared, sparking and shooting high above the battlefield. The resounding *boom* traveled like thunder over the plain as his magic sliced through the darkness.

One by one, the lights went out until the entire field was draped in an overwhelming darkness. Gavin pressed his lips together. He had to trust that his compatriots knew what to do. If they didn't…well, Gavin couldn't think about that. He had only moments to do what he needed to do to save them all and put an end to this.

Putting everything he had left to give into his attack, Gavin pulled on the threads of his magic unfurling in his veins. Fire was a costly magic that drained every last bit of energy from a sorcerer. But it was the only way to banish the fiemons.

Weak flames sputtered and flickered to life around him. Gavin concentrated on breathing life into them. Painstakingly slowly, the flames stabilized. They didn't emit much light, but they'd banished the shadows around him, leaving a clear ring where the fiemons had scrambled away.

Forcing his breaths to remain steady, Gavin licked his lips. He wished he was stronger. He *needed* to be stronger if this wasn't going to happen again. If Darshovi destroyed the gate between realms again, then they would need more than what he could reasonably sacrifice.

After all, he'd never wholly recovered from the previous war. He supposed the same could be said of Kordouva.

He wished he'd taken the Eye with him. What good was it doing in the vault? Gavin needed it here and now. Adelaide's family—and all of Kordouva—would only be safe if Gavin could manage to banish Penumbra's shadows from this realm as he had before.

But he just wasn't strong enough.

He needed more power.

Gavin clenched his jaw hard enough he feared his teeth would shatter. No matter how much he focused, the flames didn't grow.

Taking a deep breath, he forced the tension from his shoulders. Gavin resigned himself to do his best, even if it was at his expense.

What good was it to live if it meant he had to live with unsurmountable regret?

The flames flared.

What good was it to live if he hadn't given it his all, if he hadn't tried his hardest?

Licking tongues leapt and teased at the shadows. The ring of fire grew, stretching outward and upward. Gavin's heart thundered between his ears.

What good was it to live if he hadn't done all he could for love?

The heat of the flames kissed his skin. The fiemons hissed. The giant foot soldiers shrank back in an attempt to outrun the orange flames. Sparks danced on the gentle breeze that carried through the night. They winked out as they cooled, but not before they'd burned a fleeing fiemon.

Gavin urged the ring of fire to grow, to unfurl and sweep across the farm to clear a path to the house at the heart of it all. Mindful of where his forces lay and the approximate location of the house, Gavin unleashed all he had against Penumbra's scattered infantry.

All his doubts, all his fears, all his worry, every last bit of himself he could spare, he gave to the flames.

After all, hadn't he always given everything he had to ensure tomorrow's sunrise?

Emerald green eyes sparkled in his memory, just as they had every morning they'd had breakfast together. The way Adelaide's hair seemed to glow in the sunlight, giving her a soft aura. Her laugh filled his ears. And if Gavin didn't know the exhaustion in his bones, he'd believe the press of her soft lips against his was real. The memories filled his heart and eased the weight on his shoulders.

Adelaide deserved the sunrise, to live for tomorrow, even if the magic he used tonight cost him his own life. It didn't have to cost hers.

Gavin's knees shook. Even the tips of his fingers trembled. It would be a miracle if he didn't collapse. He only needed a little longer, to make certain every last fiemon, every last shadow horse and hound, had been extinguished, banished by the light.

His breaths turned ragged. Gavin peeled his eyes open, uncertain of when they'd fallen shut, and surveyed the scene around him. He squinted against the all-too-bright glare of the fire swirling around him.

Stars twinkled overhead. The heavy veil cast over the field by Penumbra's influence had lifted. The swirling bleak shadows had been extinguished. Gavin's lips pulled into a weary smile. The flames sputtered. Watching as they shrank, Gavin's knees buckled. Falling to a heap on the ground, it was all Gavin could do not to pass out as his vision swam. Grabbing blindly for his sword, Gavin tried to blink away the haze settling over his eyes. He *had* to stay awake. He still had to get to Adelaide and regroup with the knights he'd dispatched after her and Sir Maxwell, to ensure Adelaide's safety.

His limp hand knocked into the cool steel of his sword's hilt. Grasping it, Gavin leaned his weight against his sword, still stuck firmly in the ground. Taking gulps of fresh air, Gavin let his eyes flutter shut.

The *creak* and *clinking* of armor reached his ears as the Belmont knights rose and moved throughout the field. Glancing around, Gavin's eyes landed on a man rising mere feet away from him.

His eyes locked with those of the Darshovian prince.

Gone was the swirling mass of shadows that had clung to the man, the nightmare. Their absence had left nothing but a mortal man. A lean, unintimidating man who, if Gavin had to guess, was just as drained as he was, if not more so.

If fire magic was costly, then prying a portal open into another realm was fatal.

Growling, Gavin hauled himself up by his sword.

Prince Branigan matched his movements. Shadows fizzled at his fingertips.

Gavin snarled, "We both know you can't call Penumbra's shadows again."

"Just as well as you cannot draw your fire."

Every muscle in his body groaned. Gavin forced himself to pull his sword from the frozen earth. Gripping the hilt, he prepared for a duel. Across from him, the Darshovian prince drew his sword.

As his surroundings faded from Gavin's awareness, his field of vision homed in on the prince. The air crackled with tension. His arms trembled. He didn't know how well he'd be able to wield his sword, but damn it if he wouldn't try. All he had to do was survive long enough to land a killing blow to the prince.

That, and see to Adelaide's safety. Once he'd done both, Gavin could allow his body to give into the exhaustion making black dots dance on the outskirts of his vision.

Gavin drew in a deep breath. His fingers tensed around the hilt. This battle would not become a war. Not this time.

Chapter Twenty-Three

Adelaide

The carriage shuddered to a stop in front of the inn. Adelaide took a moment to compose herself before following Sir Maxwell out the door. She accepted the hand he offered her in the hopes it would offer her some stability. All she got from the gesture was a shock of cold. His skin was like ice, so unlike Gavin's touch. She wondered if it had to do with his specific type of magic—whatever that was.

"It will all be over soon, Adelaide. Try not to let your worries get to you. You need to have a clear mind right now, understand?"

Adelaide nodded. "I'm trying my best."

She looked up at the darkened inn. Acid rose in her throat as a result. She wasn't sure which was worse: the knowledge of what was awaiting her here tonight, or the knowledge that Dylan had been killed by Mistress Scrabs and her family could be next.

The subtlety of Mistress Scrabs's threats were a lot like her magic. By the time the threat was realized, it was too late. Mistress Scrabs had likely carried out the consequence she'd promised—or worse: she'd gotten hold of you.

Adelaide suppressed a shudder. She just needed to stay out of her reach and then she'd be fine. And to help Gavin save her family from whatever forces Mistress Scrabs and the prince had sent to her home, Adelaide had to stall as long as she possibly could. She set her jaw. She could do this.

She *had* to do this, for all their sakes.

Sir Maxwell led the way through the inn with his head held high. He didn't even have a sword or dagger with him. But Adelaide did, and she was grateful for it. She reached for the dagger's hilt to ensure it hadn't slipped from its sheath as Sir Maxwell opened the cellar door. Adelaide hissed.

How had the hilt gotten even hotter? She hadn't even been holding it, and even if she had, it wouldn't have been so warm as to burn her fingertips.

Sir Maxwell glanced back at her with his brows raised in question.

"Found a splinter," she whispered. "I'm fine."

His eyes swept over her skeptically before he ultimately turned away and started down the staircase. Adelaide let out a silent sigh of relief. The dagger sheathed to her side became a constant weight on her conscious mind. She couldn't help it as she found her body trying to twist away from it, fixated on the scalding heat of the hilt.

Again, Adelaide found herself wondering if it had something to do with the magic her brother had said was imbued in it. Or had she reached the point when her wits had finally abandoned her?

Adelaide took deep, steady breaths through her nose. Her temples pounded. It took every ounce of her willpower to trail after Sir Maxwell. Each step brought her deeper into the inn's underbelly and closer to her certain doom.

If they really had to hand the Eye of Behelwer into Mistress Scrabs's possession, Adelaide would never forgive herself. But at the same time, how could she stand before herself in a mirror knowing she'd sacrificed her family?

No matter what choice she made, Adelaide knew she would lose.

Sir Maxwell stopped short. Adelaide nearly tripped over her own feet in order to avoid crashing into him.

"Perhaps you'd better go first."

Adelaide gaped. "What if she asks for the Eye straight away?"

"Don't worry."

"I am, though," she sputtered. Adelaide fought to keep her voice down, but the hysteria seeping into her veins made it nearly impossible.

"Adelaide," Sir Maxwell said quietly, turning to face her and grasping her shoulders lightly. "I'm right behind you, okay? Your family will be fine. Gavin will make sure they're safe."

She nodded, unconvinced their plans would prove successful despite his earnestness. "Okay."

Nodding for her to go ahead, he smiled in a way that didn't quite reach his eyes. "Besides, they know you. If I go first, it might make them defensive. It's best not to antagonize them for now."

Adelaide swallowed. Admittedly, she knew he was right. It didn't stop the twist of fear from writhing in her gut. She doubted there was any amount of sound reasoning that could. She didn't know what she should do, or what Sir Maxwell was expecting her to do. Adelaide didn't think she could introduce him like she normally would, but neither Sir Maxwell nor Mistress Scrabs had given her any better option.

She bobbed her head firmly. Taking a step forward, Adelaide mentally prepared herself for the oncoming confrontation. Her hands clenched into fists. Her nails dug harshly into her palms. Adelaide hoped she didn't break the skin. Knowing she had little choice in the night's events, Adelaide straightened her shoulders and tried to appear as though nothing was amiss, even though her heart knew nothing was right.

The more she considered him, the more she realized how Sir Maxwell seemed detached, a fact Adelaide wished she'd realized sooner. What she had mistaken for calm was actually aloofness.

Sir Maxwell must've been someone who withdrew when he was nervous. Adelaide wanted to curse herself for not realizing it sooner. Maybe then she wouldn't have found herself stepping into the bear's den with nothing but a dagger to protect herself.

"I was beginning to wonder when you'd return, Addie." Mistress Scrabs stood from the chair they'd obviously brought down from Dylan's office and brushed her pants off. Adelaide's eyes surveyed the little room cordoned off by the crates and barrels piled in the cellar.

Where was Prince Branigan?

"Did you succeed?"

Adelaide struggled to swallow against the rock in her throat. She forced herself to look at Mistress Scrabs. Perhaps it was a good thing she didn't see the Darshovian prince. That was one less person to fight and put the odds of surviving in her favor.

It also made it easier to believe that the Eye of Behelwer wouldn't find its way into Mistress Scrabs's hands.

But his absence also grated on her heart. Had he gone out to do something horrible? Had she sent him after her family too, and not just his men?

"I…" Adelaide's mind spun. She needed to tread carefully, but her mind refused to work and put words together. There wasn't any safe way to phrase this, so she didn't hesitate a second longer. "I came with someone who claims to have the Eye."

"Oh? And who might that be?" The Master of Thieves narrowed her eyes. Static crackled in the air between them. The hair on the back of Adelaide's neck raised. It took all of her willpower not to take a step backward.

Adelaide squared her shoulders and cast a brief glance behind her. "Sir Maxwell?"

Mistress Scrabs's eyes sparkled as Sir Maxwell stepped into the light of her cellar hideaway. She slowly stood from her makeshift desk. Adelaide's eyes flitted between them, trying to gauge each of their reactions. Sir Maxwell's lips had pressed into a grim line.

"Well, isn't this something?" Mistress Scrabs said, her voice dipping into an almost sultry tone that made Adelaide frown. How was she remaining calm? "Tell me, Sir William, does Kordouva's precious White Hawk know you're here?"

"He does," Sir Maxwell said. Adelaide eyed him, catching the way his jaw twitched.

"What a pity," Mistress Scrabs huffed, leaning against the crate she'd been using as a desk and crossing her arms over her chest. "Then I suppose we'll have to deal with the archduke separately."

Adelaide's heart clenched. She clamped her lips together in an effort to stop the cry she could feel bubbling up in her chest from escaping. She needed Mistress Scrabs to believe her love for Gavin had been nothing more than a façade.

"And do *you* have what I want then?" Mistress Scrabs asked.

Silently, Sir Maxwell reached into his cloak and withdrew a wrapped bundle from within its folds. Adelaide held her breath. That couldn't really be it, could it? Had Sir Maxwell and Gavin been so foolish as to actually allow the Eye of Behelwer to leave the safety of Castle Belmont's vault? Adelaide watched in abject horror as Sir Maxwell unwrapped the small packet and revealed the legendary red-orange sunstone.

It was a clone. It had to be, right? For whatever reason, Adelaide couldn't wholly convince herself. The unease in her gut began to simmer. Bells rang between her ears like a warning toll.

Without a moment to reconsider, Adelaide harshly wrapped her hand around Sir Maxwell's arm, stopping his advance toward Mistress Scrabs.

"No."

Mistress Scrabs quirked her brow.

"No?" Mistress Scrabs asked, a cold edge to the lilt in her voice. The crackling returned as shocks of lightning *popped* in the air around Mistress Scrabs like fireflies. "Why, Adelaide, dear, I must say I'm surprised. I would have thought you wanted to ensure your family's safety."

She did.

But she couldn't. Not like this. She just had to trust that Gavin hadn't lied to her, that he was with her family at this very moment, had found the missing prince, and that the Master of Thieves had posed an empty threat, trusting in Adelaide's submission after years of being burned by her cruelty.

Adelaide slowly took the Eye into her hand. "I do. I want to see them first—to know they're safe. Then you can have the Eye."

Mistress Scrabs's smirk was too sharp. Adelaide didn't know whether or not she was alive, or if her heart had stopped beating. A sheen of cold sweat trickled down her spine, the only thing she could feel through the numbness that had consumed her.

"I see," Mistress Scrabs said slowly. "You've learned quite a lot in your years of service to me." Adelaide forced herself not to move as Mistress Scrabs took a measured step toward her. "But it wasn't enough, Addie."

Adelaide flinched. The pommel of her dagger poked her side. The heat of the metal burned her skin on contact where her shirt had ridden up. She sucked in a breath, unable to focus on one singular thing. What did Mistress Scrabs mean?

Adelaide stiffened when the Master of Thieves reached into her waistcoat pocket and pulled a familiar vial from within. "But there's one more lesson I think you should do well to learn." She held the vial of medication up teasingly. "Always have a contingency plan. People are so troublesome to manage, always thinking they know more, or can force the upper hand. You've never had it, dear Addie. And as far as I'm concerned, you've outlived your usefulness."

Adelaide held her breath. She glanced from Mistress Scrabs to the medication in her hand and back again. But Mistress Scrabs wasn't looking at her.

No, she was looking at Sir Maxwell.

"I believe this is yours, Sir Maxwell." Mistress Scrabs's words sent a chill down Adelaide's spine. "I think you can handle one thief, can't you? That is, if you want the cure for your lovely wife."

Adelaide turned to Sir Maxwell only to see that he was already facing her. His eyes shone with regret. "I'm sorry, Adelaide."

"What? Why?" she asked, taking a step away. She bumped into the crates beside her and stumbled. Sir Maxwell caught her by the wrist and attempted to pry the Eye from her hand. Her free hand formed a fist. Adelaide swung blindly, just barely catching his chin. Sir Maxwell's head knocked to the side. He didn't let go. Adelaide cried out. The hilt of the dagger had turned scalding, prodding at her side now that Sir Maxwell had her pinned against the stack of wooden crates as he tried to wrestle the Eye from her clutching fingers. She reached for the clasp of the belt that held the sheath and fumbled to undo it, hoping to rid herself of the scalding metal. "You bastard!"

As soon as the words left her mouth, the dagger cooled. Adelaide nearly sighed at the relief, but couldn't as Sir Maxwell had finally succeeded in wresting the Eye of Behelwer from her hand.

"Why?" she asked desperately. She grabbed his shoulder to keep him from turning away from her. "Why do this when you fought so hard to save Kordouva?"

Sir Maxwell didn't meet her gaze. "It's my wife," he said quietly. "She has severillik, and there was no other way to get her the medication. I…I can't live without her."

Adelaide's heart wrenched. Hadn't she done the same thing for her mother? Hadn't Mistress Scrabs preyed on her desperation too?

"You don't need them to get you the medicine," she argued. "We can figure somethi—"

"This is the price Sir Maxwell agreed to pay, Adelaide," Mistress Scrabs interrupted coolly, her tone light and factual. Everything was a transaction, a business dealing in which she stood to benefit, no matter the cost to anyone else. Adelaide's blood boiled. She'd had enough of Mistress Scrabs and the fear incited with precise words and delicate strategy. "So let him pay it. Or do you want to be responsible for his wife's death as well?"

Adelaide looked pleadingly at Sir Maxwell. Slowly, she reached for the hilt of her dagger. "Don't give her the Eye."

"I have to," Sir Maxwell muttered. "I hope you understand why. I can't…Evelynn is my everything."

Adelaide nodded. "Then I hope you understand why I can't let you."

As confusion settled on Sir Maxwell's face, Adelaide thrust the dagger forward, uncertain of where she was stabbing. She didn't want to seriously hurt Sir Maxwell, but she couldn't let him hand the Eye of Behelwer to Mistress Scrabs and damn them all.

Sir Maxwell grunted. He instantly released Adelaide, grasping the hilt. Adelaide's fingers slipped from beneath his. Acid burned her throat. Mistress Scrabs's shouted words were lost to her comprehension. All Adelaide understood was the stark shock and pain and betrayal glistening in Sir Maxwell's eyes.

"I'm sorry," she gushed. As the weight of what she'd done slammed into her, Adelaide stooped and picked the Eye up from where it had fallen between them. Taking a harried breath, she fled.

Haphazardly weaving through the maze made by the stacks of crates and groupings of barrels, Adelaide didn't look back, terrified of what she might see and sickened by the warm, tacky feeling of the blood on her hand.

Her breaths tore in and out of her.

"Adelaide!" Mistress Scrabs's voice had turned shrill. "Come back this instant!"

Nearly delirious, Adelaide almost huffed a laugh. She'd finally stood up against Mistress Scrabs, a fact neither of them had truly foreseen. And by the sound of her voice, of the crack in her words, Mistress Scrabs knew her control had slipped.

Static fizzled over Adelaide. Her skin buzzed as the current of Mistress Scrabs's magic flooded the air. But as long as she wasn't touching her, Adelaide knew she'd survive. She could ignore the static.

All she had to do was stay out of the woman's reach—and pray the range of her magic hadn't gotten stronger since the last time someone had tried to run from the Master of Thieves.

Adelaide flinched at the *bang* that echoed from above.

Her heart skipped a beat as she rounded the last of the stored goods and saw the staircase before her.

But her relief was short-lived as the prince stepped into the doorway.

The moment their eyes locked, Adelaide knew there was no escape. He knew what she had done. A shadow bloomed behind the prince, blotting out the light of the tavern above. The inky mass spilled down the stairs as Adelaide watched with wide eyes.

Not wasting a beat as he began to run down the stairs, Adelaide turned and flung herself behind a stack of crates.

Adelaide's heart sank. Mistress Scrabs had gained on her. Her nerves began to twitch against their own volition as the electric current grew stronger.

Adelaide darted between another set of crates and barrels. She doubled back to the stairs, hoping the prince had lost sight of her and run past.

"ADELAIDE!"

Her heartbeat quickened. Gavin? Boots thudded overhead. Adelaide could vaguely make out the clatter of armor-laden movements and low voices. She shoved the Eye of Behelwer down her bodice.

"I'm here!" she called out breathlessly. "The cellar!"

Relief wove its way through her veins at the promise of his arrival. Running as fast as she could, Adelaide emerged onto a clear path. Her heart swelled with hope at the sight of the stairs once more, giving her a burst of energy that she hoped would help her reach safety. Adelaide could see the shadows creeping closer to her in her peripheral vision. Drawing near enough to the stairs, Adelaide flung herself toward them in desperation.

"Ugh," she groaned. A forceful weight slammed into her, jarring her bones. She turned her head as much as she could, sprawled out on her stomach and pinned to the floor. Out of the corner of her eye, Adelaide recognized the Darshovian prince. Splinters snagged at her clothes, poking through and catching on her skin. Adelaide threw her elbow back, hoping to connect with the prince's head.

He must've dodged the blow, as all Adelaide got for her effort was the feeling she'd dislocated her shoulder blade.

"The Eye. Where is it?" he asked harshly, sitting atop her and grabbing her wrist.

Adelaide tried to blow her hair away from her face. The Eye poked painfully at the space between her breasts. Footsteps pounded down the stairwell. "You'll have to kill me to find it."

"Fine by me," he growled.

"But not by me."

Adelaide glanced up in time to see Gavin emerge in the cellar doorway. His armor gleamed in the light flooding down the stairs from the tavern above. Her eyes went wide at the power amassing in front of his outstretched hand. Belmont knights vaulted themselves over the banister and rushed forward.

Adelaide pressed herself closer to the floor and put her head down, doing her best to make herself smaller.

The Darshovian prince swore. His weight disappeared. A wave of heat soared over Adelaide's back, but not close enough to burn. Adelaide tried to ease the shuddering of her breath. Her throat burned. Panic rose up inside of her, eager to burst free. The assault of metal clashing against metal filled her ears. She refused to look up or move from her spot. She doubted she could even if she'd tried. Her limbs were anchored to the floor.

"Adelaide!" Gavin's breathless voice broke through the chaos. "Get up. We have to move."

A strong hand gripped her, pulling her up. Adelaide raised her fist. She blinked. "Gavin!"

She nearly jumped on top of him. He brushed her off, taking a firm hold of her hand and yanking her forward, pushing her toward the stairs as knights swarmed around them. "We don't have time. I have to get you to safety."

Adelaide nodded, her tongue too numb to speak. Her memory sparked. "Sir Maxwell," she tried, desperately forcing the words past her lips. With one final push, they emerged upstairs. Stumbling into the tavern with Gavin close behind her, Adelaide cleared her throat and turned her head to look at Gavin over her shoulder. Worry flooded her veins. His dull eyes were unfocused as he pushed her farther into the room. "Are you all right?"

"Fine," he panted, his lips twisted in a grimace. "Just keep going, Adelaide. You'll be safe outside."

Adelaide shook her head. "Sir Maxwell betrayed you. Mistress Scrabs promised to give him the medication if he gave her the Eye."

Gavin's brows pulled together. "Where is he now?"

Adelaide pressed her lips together. She wrung her hands together. "I…stabbed him."

Chapter Twenty-Four

Gavin

Gavin froze. His mind spun with equal parts disbelief and rage. The emotions buzzed in his veins, not unlike the feeling being near the Eye of Behelwer caused. Medication? For severillik? Gavin had known William all his life. He was nearly unsusceptible to all illnesses. Healing magic ran through his veins as strongly as light magic ran through Gavin's. William had been at his side all through Penumbra's War. Why would he betray Kordouva—their friendship—now?

Realization dawned on Gavin.

William's wife, Evelynn, had been sick since before they left to find the Eye. William had never told him it was severillik, but it all made sense now, why William couldn't fully heal her.

Gavin forced himself to ask the question that could shatter his entire world. "And the Eye? Where is it now?"

Adelaide glanced at her feet. "I have it," she said slowly as she continued to fidget.

Gavin's curiosity piqued.

"It's…I had to tuck it someplace safe!" she explained, her voice higher in pitch than usual.

Gavin raised his brows and opened his mouth to ask where before he understood what Adelaide was indicating. His eyes traveled down the curves of her body and flitted back to her face. Coughing, he ducked his head and willed his eyes away from her. His head throbbed with the movement, protesting against every slight change of scene or demand Gavin made of it. He feared he'd fall to the ground and never wake up before this fight was over.

"Here." Adelaide's quiet voice blasted through the heavy exhaustion bearing down on Gavin's body.

Gavin's eyes fixed on the rough, deep orange stone in Adelaide's palm. Surely, William hadn't taken the real Eye of Behelwer with them. Surely, this was all a mistake. Adelaide wouldn't know the difference, and it would've bought them *some* time to save her family. Urgency bubbled up in his blood. The stone called to him, to the magic simmering in his veins.

"Damn." He gently grasped the stone. A surge of power welled up inside of him. Gavin sucked in a breath.

"Adelaide," he said, his throat dry. "I need you to run from here, as quickly as you can, and don't stop until you reach Castle Belmont. Can you do that?"

"Why?" she asked, her eyes wide. "What are you going to do?"

Gavin tamped down his magic, hoping to leash it long enough to comfort Adelaide—and avoid the risk of regret before it was too late. Cupping her face, he stroked his thumb across her cheek. His eyes dipped, studying her lips for a heartbeat. "I need to know you'll be safe before I go back down there and end any chance that Mistress Scrabs and Prince Branigan will succeed."

Too soon, he pulled away. If he didn't now, he never would. Gavin knew that.

Swallowing against the bitterness sitting in his throat, he urged her to run once more.

Before he could turn and walk away, Adelaide grabbed his arm, forcing him to stay put. Gavin opened his mouth to tell her to go, to order her to leave and find safety, but found only Adelaide's lips crashing into his.

He melted against the contact, savoring the softness of her lips, and dragged her closer, deepening the kiss.

Adelaide pulled away first, turning her cheek before he could press his lips to hers once more, her chest heaving. Her grip on his collar tightened, keeping him from moving—not that he'd had any intention of doing so. He delicately brushed away stray strands of Adelaide's hair, running his hand through it, and gently twirled the soft curl around his finger, completely unaware and unburdened by the war raging on in the cellar below their feet.

He'd done enough fighting in his life already. He'd sacrificed more than enough for Kordouva. Why couldn't he indulge himself just this once?

Adelaide's brilliant green eyes slowly met his. Her words made his heart sink. "Promise me you'll be careful, Gavin. I don't want to know life without you."

"I love you too, Adelaide," he said, swallowing against the sinking realization her words had brought to the forefront of his mind. This moment couldn't last.

He was Kordouva's White Hawk.

Leaning closer to press a firm kiss between her brows, Gavin slowly slipped his arms from around her waist and up to rest on her shoulders. Adelaide's emerald eyes had filled with tears. "I'll see you back home at Castle Belmont. Your family is already there, safe and unharmed."

She nodded, wiping her eyes. "Thank you. I don't know how—"

He interrupted, "There isn't anything I wouldn't do to see you smile, to know you're safe, and know you're right where you belong. So leave, before it's too late and I can't fight the Eye's call any longer."

Adelaide took a breath. Her shoulders rose and fell with it, grounding Gavin to this moment and helping him focus on her instead of the tempting allure of the Eye of Behelwer.

"Home," she repeated slowly, as if testing the word on her tongue. A small smile played on her lips. "I'll be waiting for you at home then, however long it takes."

Gavin grinned. Pressing one last kiss to Adelaide's cheek, he gave in to the pull of reality. Magic roared in his veins, bolstered by the Eye of Behelwer in his hand.

"I won't be long," he assured her, finally letting go so she could slip away and find safety. "I promise."

Never again would he let something keep him from his loved ones, from his home. Never again would he feel his heart tear in two like this, watching as Adelaide turned and ran through the open door, fleeing into the night.

Gavin promised he would never have to make the choice between duty and love ever again, for himself, for Adelaide, for whatever their futures held.

He closed his eyes. His heart kept an irrelevant time, beating furiously until Gavin gained control of the forces acting upon him and organized the chaos in his mind.

If he was to successfully wield his power and control the Eye's influence over it, he needed to focus. His heartbeat slowed. Settling into a steady rhythm, his heart beat like a war drum.

Gavin straightened. He threw his shoulders back and stalked toward the cellar door. Gavin tightened his fingers around the Eye. His heart thrummed in his chest. His temples pounded. His power had hit a crescendo, and gone was the exhaustion of wielding the unruly fire magic earlier in the night.

At the base of the stairs, a Belmont knight worked furiously to save William from his injuries. Gavin paused for a moment, studying William's reddened face, puckered and blistered from what could only be Mistress Scrabs's electric powers, and blood-soaked tunic from where Adelaide had stabbed him.

Gavin's lips twisted into a frown. Torn between wanting to see his best friend survive and never wanting to see him again, Gavin carried on. Magic flared between the stacked barrels and crates. The clash of metal against metal assaulted his ears. He didn't know what to think about the fact that the fight wasn't over. Shouldn't it have been by now?

Or was Mistress Scrabs that formidable?

Gavin caught sight of a finely dressed woman over the top of a pile of crates. Her once-elegant clothes were in tatters around her. One side of her waistcoat had been torn or sliced, creating a tail that skewed toward one side, trailing on the ground behind her as she battled furiously against three knights. Magic crackled around her. It sparked between her hands, arcing with her movements as she sliced and countered her opponents. He gritted his teeth as the knight fell to the ground, jerking this way and that as the current buzzed through him.

The Darshovian prince was nowhere in sight. Gavin knew he still lived and breathed, as evident by the inky shadows writhing between the stored wares and the sounds of the knights' scuffle to subdue him. He paid their battle no mind. Shadows were a familiar foe.

But Mistress Scrabs wasn't. Her magic was new and as rare as the ability to wield fire.

Moreover, Mistress Scrabs had hurt Adelaide and evaded him for four years.

She was his target.

Gavin reached up and quickly undid the straps holding his armor in place. Each piece fell with a clatter. Each layer of metal he shed, the better Gavin felt. Mistress Scrabs wouldn't use his own armor to her advantage.

His task done, Gavin stalked forward. Power amassed at the tips of Gavin's fingers. He continued forward at a measured pace, stalking around the crates as threads of light radiated like a halo from his hand.

Gathering the strands and sparks, he molded them into a ball. The Eye buzzed, as if humming in eager approval. Gavin launched his attack with a forceful thrust of his hand. Another ball of light began to form before the first had even left his grasp. He calmly watched it soar toward the Master of Thieves.

Either feeling its heat or seeing its glow, Mistress Scrabs turned toward it at the last moment and dove out of the way before the orb could make impact. Gavin didn't hesitate. Hurling the second one at her, Gavin barely registered the Belmont knights slinking away.

"Go and fetch the prince," he ordered, not once taking his eyes off of Mistress Scrabs as she panted, her shoulders rounded with exhaustion. She watched him wearily. "I'll handle this."

Mistress Scrabs wiped the sweat from her lips with the back of her hand. She huffed a laugh. "What took you so long, Archduke? Aren't I worthy of your time?"

Gavin shrugged. "No more than any other traitor to Kordouva."

She pressed a hand to her heaving chest, frowning insincerely. "Your words are harsh, Archduke."

He studied the lines of her face, trying to strip away her mask and finally unveil the woman behind this criminal empire. Were his suspicions right? Had Adelaide singled out the right portrait?

"Haven't you ever wanted something more than this, more than being the White Hawk?" Mistress Scrabs went on. Gavin tuned back to her words. His brow arched. "I think you'd look quite charming in a crown."

"And you by my side?" he guessed. He rolled his eyes. "I'd rather fight Penumbra's shadows for eternity."

Mistress Scrabs's face fell, her features stricken beneath her mask. She shook her head, quickly recovering her composure in spite of the fraying of her hair and the obvious weight of exhaustion settled on her shoulders.

"I see." She clicked her tongue. "Then I suppose you liked His Highness's gift earlier."

Gavin didn't respond. He flexed his hand. His magic surged inside of him, pressing against his skin in an effort to burst free of his body.

The Eye of Behelwer cooled in his palm.

Gritting his teeth, Gavin unleashed his magic. Thick tendrils of light unfurled from his raised hand. Fractals of light pulled from the air and joined the bolt surging toward Mistress Scrabs. Her eyes glowed with fear in the light. Hastily, she threw herself to the side.

But she wasn't fast enough.

Gavin's magic slammed into her and sent her flying backward. Crates splintered and cracked, toppling onto her.

Gavin cautiously approached the smoldering pile. Any static the air had held had disappeared. Standing over the pile, Gavin watched the Master of Thieves carefully. Her breath had turned ragged and slow. She showed no signs of moving.

Maybe it was wrong, but Gavin couldn't help but feel disappointed. He'd finally been given a valid reason to explore the Eye's capabilities, and Mistress Scrabs hadn't even stood long enough to fight him.

He stooped to haul her from the wreckage. His hand had hardly wrapped around her arm when Mistress Scrabs's eyes burst open.

Pure pain licked at his veins. Static seized his blood and wiped all thought from his mind. Gavin fought to keep his balance. Blinking rapidly, he willed his fingers to release their hold, to break the contact between him and Mistress Scrabs.

A growl vibrated in his chest, different from the sensation of the *statique trosher* that swept through his body. The Eye dug into his other hand as his grip tightened.

Inch by inch, Gavin regained control of his body.

He glanced down at Mistress Scrabs. With a smirk he said, "Is that all you can do?"

Her face went slack.

Gavin hauled her to her feet, ignoring the subtle ripple of static still in his blood. He didn't know why she bothered anymore. It was obvious her magic had no effect on him. A knight came over and handed Gavin a pair of handcuffs engraved with markings that would suppress her magic. He quickly clasped them around her wrists, and the faint buzz stopped.

Before the knight could take her away, Gavin stopped him, saying he would like a moment alone.

He waited a beat for the Belmont knights to collect Prince Branigan from his unconscious heap on the floor and drag him away. Gavin held Mistress Scrabs's glare, unbothered by the venom in her eyes as silence descended on the cellar for the first time all night.

"Every ounce of suffering you've caused Adelaide, I will make sure is repaid tenfold." Mistress Scrabs's eyes widened in panic. Gavin hummed, tilting his head, and relished the fear in her features. He smirked. "And to think, all this because you wanted power." He leaned forward and ripped her mask from her face.

Mistress Scrabs gasped, and turned her face away in an attempt to hide, but Gavin didn't let her. He grabbed her chin and forced her to face him.

"Was being a baroness beneath you, Lady Alyton?"

Chapter Twenty-Five

Adelaide

Adelaide carelessly threw the door to the sitting room open. Her eyes swept over the room. Breathless, she clung to the solid door, afraid her grip would splinter the wood.

"Adelaide!" Her father rose from the couch in front of the fireplace. Relief swept over his harried features, easing the stiffness of his shoulders.

"Papa!" Adelaide's lip wobbled. She sucked in a breath and crumpled to her knees. Heaving a sob, Adelaide buried her face in her hands. Overwhelming relief raged like a snowstorm inside her mind. But there was that frost, that chill that came with the flurries. It was the worry that tugged on her heartstrings.

What exactly had she left behind?

Would Gavin be able to subdue Mistress Scrabs and Prince Branigan? Or would the Eye of Behelwer fall into their hands despite all their efforts?

Strong arms wrapped around her. Adelaide returned the embrace and clung to her father.

"It's all my fault," she whispered.

Her father shushed her.

"I'm sure the archduke will be all right, Addie," her mother said. Her voice was hoarse and frail. Adelaide risked a glance at her. Covered in blankets and sitting close to the flames, Adelaide realized she'd failed at providing the medication in time. Her mother's condition had worsened, and if she didn't…

Her father squeezed her tighter, as if his embrace could still the trembling in her bones.

Adelaide searched for Ethan's hazel eyes. A hard look met her gaze. He nodded his head. Adelaide forced herself to take a deep breath and pull away from her father. Wiping her eyes, she swallowed the rest of her tears and fears.

"I'm glad you're all safe and here," she said, forcing a smile.

"Addie," Amber started, frowning slightly as she tilted her head, "how come the Archduke came to save us?"

"Amber," Papa chastised. Adelaide stared at her sister, struck by the question. Her brain scrambled for an answer, certain Amber wasn't the only one wondering the same thing.

Well, maybe not Ethan. Adelaide knew without a shadow of a doubt that Ethan had already guessed the reason for Gavin's involvement. The only thing left to explain was their relationship. The tips of Adelaide's ears burned.

It had all been real. The only ruse, she realized, was the idea that what was between them was an act at all.

"It's all right," Adelaide said. Sniffling, she added, "I'm sure you'd all like an explanation."

Slowly standing, Adelaide let her eyes fall shut. "I…I haven't been honest with you."

"Addie," Ethan said in warning.

"No." She shook her head. "I can't live with this burden anymore."

Adelaide's heart kept count of the seconds ticking by. Her parents sat together on the couch. Her father held her mother in his arms, his lips pressed tightly together. Adelaide wouldn't say they were pursed, but they weren't necessarily a frown either. Nonetheless, the disappointment on his face was eminent. Amber tried to make conversation, asking questions about Castle Belmont like how many balls Adelaide thought Gavin had held or if there were any upcoming and could they attend them too?

Her mother stared into the fireplace with dull eyes, occasionally dozing off. The only thing she'd said after Adelaide had finished her tale of how she'd been a thief for Mistress Scrabs and how they'd been able to get the medicine was that she was sorry.

Adelaide didn't know whether she wanted to laugh or cry more. Her mother was sorry? For what, being sick?

What Adelaide couldn't fully understand was how readily her parents had taken the blame upon themselves. They'd known she was involved in something all along. The only shock to them was how involved she was in the black market. They'd assumed she was merely purchasing the medication. The shock and horror her confession had brought would remain with Adelaide until her last breath. Never once had it crossed their minds that their daughter was a thief for the worst of people, or that she could be considered an accessory to smuggling the medication in from Darshovi—to treason.

All it had taken was one night, and her entire world had shattered. Her secrets, her heart, her treason.

Adelaide clasped and unclasped her hands. Her eyes strayed to the door more often than she'd ever admit to. She tried to placate her mind with the idea that it was because she couldn't sit and wait in the uncomfortable silence that had descended upon the sitting room in the wake of her confession. But the small voice that dwelled in the shadows of her mind knew the true reason behind her impatience.

She was waiting for Gavin to walk through the door. She wanted to see with her own eyes that he was all right. She needed to hear from his lips that he was unharmed. And even more selfishly, Adelaide needed to know what had happened or would happen to Mistress Scrabs.

"The Archduke…" Adelaide's eyes snapped to her mother as she sat up, coughing. Adelaide rushed to her side, taking the seat on her other side as her father braced her mother in his arms. "He knows of all this as well?"

Adelaide hesitated, glancing down at her hands. Her mother's boney hands grasped hers in a cold hold.

"Adelaide," she said, her voice as frail as her grip, "does he make you happy?"

Did he? Was that what she felt? If so, did that explain the restlessness she'd experienced waiting for him day in and day out as he attended to matters of state?

"I…I enjoy his company…" she replied slowly. Her brows furrowed in concentration. "He's quiet, but…" she smiled softly, "I don't mind it. It's natural rather than stifling, and he doesn't overwhelm my space. It's like we can just be, and it's…"

Wonderful.

"You had better sort your feelings out quickly, Addie," Ethan called from the window. "There're horses coming up the drive and a carriage."

Adelaide's mind came to a crashing halt. Ethan's words echoed in her ears. The beating of her own heart or the breath in her lungs faded from her consciousness. Relief and terror battled against each other for control over her mind. Adrenaline made her a specter in her own body. A fuzzy static filled Adelaide's ears. Desperation gave her wings as she jumped to her feet and bolted from the room, past timeless paintings and down winding halls.

The fresh night air brought Adelaide back to her senses. The galloping of the horses' hooves drowned out the thrum of panic and helplessness in her blood. Adelaide forced herself to a stop on the stone steps leading up into Castle Belmont. The group came right up to the steps, but with their armor and cloaks, they all looked the same in the dim moonlight. Adelaide tried not to look disappointed as each soldier dismounted in turn and Gavin hadn't been revealed to her. Instead, she fought to appear calm, as if she hadn't sprinted through the halls of the prestigious Belmont Estate in a strange mix of panic and excitement.

"Lady," a knight bobbed his head in greeting, "His Grace will only be a moment."

Before Adelaide could ask if Gavin was all right, the knight had left and joined the tangle around the carriage. Resigned to waiting and watching, Adelaide wrapped her arms around herself and attempted to rub the cold from her skin. The chill in the air had finally sunk into her bones and broke through the chaos of her mind.

Light flickered around the carriage—magic. Adelaide's breath caught in her throat. A pair of knights broke away from the cluster as the carriage door was wrenched open by another. Caught by the magical illumination, Adelaide took in the disheveled black hair and fur-lined cloak that occasionally adorned her shoulders.

"Gavin," she breathed.

Without a care for what was happening at the carriage or the position he was in, Adelaide rushed forward. As she came upon them, their soft words disappeared, and the dame Gavin was speaking with returned to the scene surrounding the carriage. Gone was his armor, and with it, all of Adelaide's fears and the threat against Kordouva.

"Gavin!" Adelaide called, desperate to see him before he could turn away.

He turned toward her sharply. There wasn't any time for words as she flung herself at him and wrapped her arms around his neck. She breathed him in, relishing the comforting scent of his skin. Clenching her jaw to keep the tears stinging her eyes at bay, Adelaide buried her face in the crook of his neck. The fur of his cloak tickled her cheek and bare arms.

Gavin inhaled sharply.

"I'm sorry!" Adelaide gushed, pulling back. "Are you hurt? Do you need help? Can I—"

Gavin gently took her face between his hands. "I'm fine. Exhausted, but unharmed."

Adelaide sagged in relief and leaned into his touch. "I'm glad to hear it."

"What are you doing out here, Adelaide?" he asked, slowly withdrawing his hands from her face. Adelaide nearly whined. She wanted nothing more than to keep the contact between them and steal the warmth of his touch. Gavin wrapped his arms around her, drawing his cloak around her as he did and squeezed her tightly. "Please tell me you haven't been waiting outside for me all this time."

She shook her head. "I haven't been. Ethan saw you coming from the window, and I…I had to see you."

"Let's go inside. It's been a long night."

Adelaide peeked over his shoulder. A litter leaned against the carriage. In the distance, she could just make out six figures walking toward the archway that led to the estate's back courtyard.

And Castle Belmont's barracks.

Gavin rubbed her back, a vain attempt at soothing the tension that had seeped into her muscles.

"It's over, Adelaide." His voice, despite being soft and comforting, didn't allow space for any argument. "You and your family are safe. Mistress Scrabs and the Den of Thieves are no more. Prince Branigan will be dealt with, and Sir Maxwell will recover from his injuries."

"And then what?"

"Well," Gavin smiled faintly, "I was thinking we could sleep in and have a quiet breakfast and…oh, you meant for them?"

A laugh crackled up from Adelaide's chest. Quickly catching herself, she stifled it behind her hand.

Gavin's smile turned into a grin. He gently pulled her hand away and pressed a lingering kiss to her knuckles that made her cheeks warm.

"If I may say so," Gavin said, pulling her impossibly closer with a slight tug on their joined hands. The arm around her waist tightened, but only for a moment. "I think your heart has been burdened enough.

Don't worry about them any longer, Adelaide. As of tonight, your life is your own again."

Adelaide stared up at him. A glint of sadness swept over Gavin's eyes. Slowly, his hand slipped from hers, and the arm around her waist began to retract.

"What would you like to do now, Adelaide? The choice is yours."

Adelaide caught his arm and grabbed at his collar. "I want to kiss you. I want this to last, to be real. I want *you*, Gavin. All of you, if you'll have all of me…even though I…I think I committed treason—to save my mother."

The beat of silence pounded ominously against Adelaide's chest. Gavin's clear blue eyes held hers, indiscernible.

Nearly driven to madness, Adelaide's grip began to falter.

Her heart sank. She'd been wrong. No matter what Gavin felt for her, it wasn't enough to save what could be. Her treachery was too big of an obstacle to overcome.

"I know," he said quietly.

"You…you do?" Adelaide blinked. Her mind and all her heart's intentions stilled.

"The day you went to visit your family," Gavin explained, slowly taking her hand in his, "I followed you. I saw your mother, and I realized how badly the illness had run its course and knew the only way she could survive it was if she had the medicine from Darshovi."

Adelaide shook her head. "If you knew all this time, then…"

"I didn't care." Gavin cupped her cheek. The night's chill rushed through the break in their defense as the cloak shifted with his movement. Adelaide shivered. "I would have done the same thing, if not more. I would've waged a war against the gods if doing so would bear even the slightest chance of saving someone I love."

"So what happens now then, if you already knew?"

"This." He smiled, bringing his other hand up to hold her face between his hands.

Adelaide tilted her face up. Her heart fluttered. Gavin's lips hesitantly met hers. Adelaide pressed herself closer, desperate to feel him. Wrapping her arms around his neck, Adelaide parted her lips. Warmth spread through her, washing away years of fear and doubt. She hummed, playing with the short lock of hair at the nape of Gavin's neck.

Gavin groaned and nipped at her bottom lip. His hands squeezed her hips.

Panting, Adelaide pulled back. Gavin rested his forehead on hers, and Adelaide was tempted to kiss him again. Her mind nagged at her. There was still too much to talk about, and far too much to sort through before she could wholly indulge herself in moments like this.

"Stay here," Gavin begged.

"I want to," Adelaide breathed. "but what will people think? What am I supposed to do?"

"Damn them." Gavin stroked her cheek with his thumb, parting just enough to look deeply into her eyes. "All that matters to me is if you'll be happy here…with me. You can do as you please, whenever you please. Just…stay?"

Dizzy with emotion, Adelaide couldn't focus. A single word sat on her tongue, eager and bursting with energy. She wanted to set it free, to have Gavin sweep her off her feet and for the sun to rise, smiling brightly, in the morning. But the ashes in her stomach stirred. She couldn't dispel the writhing shadows in her gut. For so long…

She'd lived someone else's life.

Tears threatened Adelaide's eyes once more.

She wanted tomorrow.

"I'd like that." She smiled. "I'll stay."

Gavin's face went slack, shocked for a moment, before a dazzling grin painted his features. He lifted her with ease and spun her around.

Adelaide laughed. Uncaring of the world around them, she leaned down and kissed him once more.

"I'll gladly stay if it means being with you," she murmured as they broke apart and Gavin set her back on her feet. Eyes closed, Gavin bent down and leaned his forehead against hers as if relieved by her words. Clinging to each other, Adelaide let her eyes fall shut. She breathed him in—the scent of him, his sweat, the hint of his soap, and fine leather—content to just be.

"I don't care what happens tomorrow," Gavin said quietly. His breath fanned over her lips like a phantom kiss. "I only care about this, you, right here."

Adelaide smiled, nudging her nose against his. "And here I was finally looking forward to tomorrow."

Gavin laughed. Pulling away slowly, he unclasped his cloak and draped it over her shoulders. He laced their fingers together. Slowly, he led her from the driveway and up the front steps. "I'll gladly walk into tomorrow for you." Adelaide quirked her brow, which only caused Gavin to grin brightly, the corners of his eyes creasing. "I had wanted to freeze this moment."

Adelaide shook her head, smiling to herself. "That would've been okay too."

Gavin squeezed her hand. Adelaide returned the gesture, letting him guide her through the halls of Castle Belmont. The night's chill slowly faded from her bones. Exhaustion wove its way through her bloodstream. Her limbs grew heavy the farther they walked. Adelaide looped her arm around Gavin's to support herself, glad he was there to lean on as they finally made it back to the sitting room where she'd left her family. Gavin stopped, causing Adelaide to follow suit.

"I've asked Thomas and Elizabeth to prepare some rooms for your family. We can sort things out tomorrow."

Adelaide hummed in agreement. "You never did answer me," she said, slowly rounding on Gavin to face him. "What will happen to Sir Maxwell? To me?"

Gavin took a breath. "I'm not sure. I've sent a message to the king to tell him of Mistress Scrabs's and Prince Branigan's capture." Pausing, he grasped her other hand. Grounded by the contact, Adelaide held on to her waning patience. "Jameson is fair, and if I explain all that's happened…"

"But you're not sure," Adelaide interrupted. She nodded her head slowly. Not even Gavin could protect her from the king's rule.

"No," he said, "but I know my cousin. I believe he'll listen to me.

You kept the Eye of Behelwer safe. Both you and Sir Maxwell were coerced by Mistress Scrabs. Jameson will see reason, that I'm sure of."

"Don't sacrifice your standing for me," she begged. "I've always known the consequences for my actions."

"I wouldn't be sacrificing myself. I would be telling the truth to my king as a loyal subject who's done quite a lot to secure his throne."

His response darted around Adelaide's mind. Her brows furrowed. "Do you intend to blackmail the king?"

"I wouldn't think of it like that," Gavin said, his voice full of humor as he considered her question. "I would see it more as me reminding him of my service and defending the actions of two Kordouvians subjected to a cruel and horrible illness and the lack of an ethical cure."

Adelaide shook her head in disbelief. "I'll wait to pack my bags then."

"Ah," Gavin teased, "so you intended to run? I should warn you—I'm very good at finding things and people."

"Hm," Adelaide said, "so does that mean you wouldn't come with me if I'd asked? "

"Would you ask me?" Gavin countered.

Adelaide's heart fluttered as Gavin's eyes darkened with a storm of mystery and a burning intensity that captivated her. Like a vow, she said, "I would."

Chapter Twenty-Six

Gavin

I would.

The simple vow echoed in Gavin's ears, keeping time with his footfalls against the marble floor of the palace's grand foyer. He strode through the cavernous space just as he had a million times before. Nothing had changed. The same suits of armor stood at attention along the walls. The same battle-weary shields hung on the wall, representing all the households that had fought alongside their sovereign during Penumbra's War. The early morning light illuminated the hall just the same as it always did this time of year, so why did it feel different? Why did he feel out of place here?

Gavin swallowed, forcing his feet down the next hall and toward Jameson's study.

It was Adelaide, and the concern twisting through his heart that had muted his confidence.

His temples throbbed with the beginnings of a headache. The door to Jameson's office taunted him from the end of the hall.

Gavin replayed the speech he'd rehearsed in his head over again. He hoped it was enough to save Adelaide and minimize William's punishment for betraying them. After all, they'd been through too much together to wholly condemn William.

Not one to keep the king waiting, Gavin forced himself to knock.

"Enter," his cousin's bored voice drawled, muffled by the solid door.

Drawing a sharp breath as he let himself in, Gavin sent up a silent prayer to gods he didn't truly believe in until now. He couldn't fight and win his way through this obstacle. He couldn't even outsmart it. All he could do was hope Jameson would listen to him, and give him the respect to consider his speech.

That was all.

Never had he felt this helpless or useless in the act of protecting those he cared about.

Jameson sat behind his large wooden desk, shifting through a pile of papers. A quill hung awkwardly in between his fingers.

"They never tell you how much paperwork looms behind the crown," he grumbled. Glancing over the rim of his reading glasses, his eyes studied Gavin from head to toe. "What's wrong? You look like you've swallowed a frog."

"Just a long night, Your Majesty."

Jameson clicked his tongue. His eyes narrowed as he set the papers down and took off his glasses, setting all of it aside. "You only ever use my title when something's wrong."

Gavin clenched his jaw. How could he forget how well they knew each other? They grew up together, they fought together, and gods if they hadn't survived together.

"Is it about William? Because then I could understand why you're making that face." Jameson waved his hand dismissively. "If it's not, then you'll have to explain it to me. Not only did you succeed in discovering the Master of Thieves and detaining her, but you captured Darshovi's fifth prince as well—and all in one night. I think that's something worth celebrating even in spite of William's…misguided judgement."

"It's not just William," Gavin finally said, licking his lips. "I've fallen in love."

Jameson arched his brow. "I fail to see the cause for the haunted frown on your face."

Gavin took a deep breath. "She was an agent of Mistress Scrabs's sent to steal the Eye of Behelwer…and then my heart."

"Which did she steal first?" Jameson asked, amused. "I would say it was your heart, as I already know it was William who took the sunstone."

"She was acting under duress." Gavin struggled to maintain his composure. His thoughts scattered. This wasn't at all how he planned to discuss Adelaide's situation.

"How so? She was a thief. She worked for Mistress Scrabs. I see no—"

"All true, but there's more than what your spies and informants can dredge up if you would just listen to me," Gavin burst.

Jameson sat back in his chair. As they stared at each other, Gavin didn't know whether he'd just joined Adelaide and William as an enemy of the kingdom, or if his cousin would finally let him speak unencumbered by his preconceived notions. Jameson sat back, essentially lounging in his desk chair, and waved a hand for Gavin to proceed. "All right. Tell me, who's the woman you've fallen in love with?"

Gavin blinked in disbelief. His cousin was actually going to exercise the patience the situation called for? "Her name is Adelaide, and she's…

quiet and smart. She's kind too. It's strange, but when I'm with her, I feel comfortable. It's like she's the embodiment of peace."

"So," Jameson interrupted, "Adelaide is the reason why you're suddenly a poet?"

Gavin glared at him. His cousin raised his hands in surrender. "All right, forgive me for making a joke. Carry on. Tell me why you feel the need to plead Adelaide's case."

Gavin went on to tell Jameson everything Adelaide had told him, and filled in his theories for what she hadn't. He told him of her family, and even the medication Lady Alyton had smuggled into Kordouva that Adelaide accepted as payment for her thievery. He finished by telling Jameson about how it was Adelaide that had ensured the Eye's safety and returned it to him.

When he was done, the king was silent. Long moments stretched by before he said anything at all. In the time that lapsed between them, stifled by quiet, Gavin fought against the itch to tap his fingers against his leg, to move, to dispel the adrenaline coursing through him.

"I never asked for any of this, for the burden of making decisions." Jameson blew out a breath and rubbed his temple. "I was supposed to live a quiet life and maybe consent to a political marriage, but never was I supposed to rule." He paused, and for the first time in their lives,

Gavin saw the burden Jameson shouldered. He could ride into battle unencumbered and unafraid, but decisions of state, the weight of the crown, had been as detrimental to Jameson as all of his errands had been to Gavin. Finally, Jameson focused on him once more. "That's still quite the account of criminal activity, Gavin."

Gavin opened his mouth to protest, to reiterate that Adelaide hadn't acted of her own free will. Jameson cast him a withering look reserved for petulant council members and held up a hand that made Gavin swallow hard.

"But I understand." Jameson stood and crossed the room to the fireplace. Bracing a hand against the mantel, he added, "This is a difficult position. Even though Lady Alyton forced Adelaide to steal for her, Adelaide still aided and abetted her. Then there's the fact that she willfully accepted smuggled goods."

"I see," Gavin said. He stood and pulled the envelope from his waistcoat's inner pocket. "Well, I've said what I've needed to and believe my report is sufficient enough. I'll leave you to your deliberations."

Gavin watched, wide-eyed, as Jameson threw his report in the fireplace. Flames erupted around the paper and licked at the envelope's edges until it caught fire. Baffled, Gavin shook his head and addressed his cousin.

"What are you planning?" Gavin asked.

"Hopefully, a wedding." Jameson grinned. Turning serious again, he added, "Now sit. We have much to discuss about what happens next. The people need the medication, but I can't condone its creation. How do we provide for our people without causing the suffering of others?"

Chapter Twenty-Seven

Adelaide

Adelaide squinted against the sunlight. She stared up at Castle Belmont and wrapped her arms around herself. Gavin hadn't returned from his trip to the palace yet. Every minute dragged on and drove Adelaide closer and closer to the edge of madness.

All he'd offered her before he'd left was a lingering kiss that seemed more like an apology than a happy parting of ways.

Unable to sit still, Adelaide gave up on keeping her family company and had left Amber to her embroidery, her mother to her nap, and her father to a game of checkers with Ethan. That's how Adelaide had found herself pacing in front of the bronze statue of the first Hughes to reside at Castle Belmont situated in the center of the estate's front courtyard.

The bitter cold burned her nostrils. A brisk wind blew down from the mountain peaks in the distance, disturbing the valley they guarded. Every so often, Adelaide swore she saw a snowflake sparkle in the sunlight.

Rubbing the cold from her fingers, Adelaide turned back toward the castle. She couldn't wait outside any longer. Even with her warm cloak, the cold had succeeded in slipping into her bones. There was no way of knowing how much longer Gavin would be.

Resigned, she mounted the steps. Reaching for the door handle, Adelaide cast one last look at the driveway, willing Gavin to appear on the horizon.

Adelaide's breath caught in her throat. A lone figure appeared in the distance. She squinted. Her heartbeat quickened. As each passing second brought the figure closer, Adelaide made out a horse and rider. The rider's cloak rippled behind them. Adelaide's eyes widened as she realized the cloak flapping in the wind was navy blue.

Gavin.

Frozen in place, Adelaide held her breath, counting the seconds until she could make out his features. She knew the moment he saw her standing on the porch, for he sat up straighter and urged his horse into a gallop. Gravel flew into the air until Gavin finally came to a stop before the steps leading up into Castle Belmont. Desperately searching for any sign that would indicate how his meeting with the king went, she received no hint.

An attendant brushed past her. Adelaide bit the inside of her cheek. She shifted on her feet as she watched Gavin give his horse a pat and soothed his mane before handing the reins to the attendant. Not wasting a moment between the second the reins had passed from him to the attendant, Gavin bounded up the steps and finally smiled at her.

"Let's go inside," he said simply.

Adelaide nodded her head. Accepting Gavin's arm, she battled against the questions assaulting her mind. Gavin clearly wanted to tell her once they were someplace warm, and Adelaide didn't entirely mind that. What she *did* mind was the suspense bubbling up inside of her which made it difficult for her to breathe.

Luckily, Gavin didn't bring her far. Leading her into the first room with a door he could close, Gavin turned to her and grinned.

She looked at him expectantly, her mouth too dry to speak. Did this mean what she thought it did? Had the king pardoned her?

As if reading her mind, Gavin nodded.

Air rushed back into Adelaide's lungs. She threw her arms around Gavin, grateful that he'd caught her in her excitement.

Breaking apart, she gushed, "How? What did you say to him? What about Sir—"

"Can't we just enjoy this moment?" Gavin asked, trailing his fingertips down her cheek.

Adelaide shivered, her chest rising and falling with each breath. Melting under his warm gaze, she nodded. "But you'll tell me?"

"Later. Right now, I just want to be with you."

Watching the flames, Adelaide let the steady rhythm of Gavin's heartbeat consume her. The silence between them was filled with the crackle of the fire, the beating of their hearts, and all the thoughts she wasn't able to squash.

But for one beautiful moment, it had all stopped. The tips of Adelaide's ears burned remembering the searing kiss they'd shared. She hadn't wanted it to end. She didn't want *this* to end. Content just lying in his arms and breathing in the scent of him and relishing the softness of his shirt against her cheek, Adelaide began to wonder if it mattered what had happened with the king. All she knew for certain was that she was right where she wanted to be.

Gavin shifted beneath her. As he began to rub her back, Adelaide glanced up only to find him already watching her with soft eyes.

"So…what did he decide then?"

"That if no crime was committed, then no judgement was needed."

"But—"

"We decided no one needed to know about your involvement. As far as any official report is concerned, you were never involved with Lady Alyton or her Den of Thieves."

"So…I've been absolved of all crimes?"

"Yes."

Adelaide let out a breath. She shouldn't go looking for leaks in a ship when there weren't any. Still, she asked, "And that's legal?"

"Jameson is the king, and it was his idea, so I suppose it is. Why? Are you worried he'll change his mind?"

Was she?

Adelaide curled her fingers against Gavin's chest. Her mind couldn't quite comprehend it all. "I'm not sure. I guess, just after all that's happened, I thought…"

She trailed off, uncertain of what it was she still feared and what she hadn't. All fears had come to pass, and neither she nor her family had suffered in its course.

Adelaide pushed herself up to hover over Gavin. "What does that mean for us?"

“I’m hoping,” Gavin said, stroking her arms, “it means you’ll stay.”

“I thought that was decided already,” Adelaide teased.

“I suppose it was.” Gavin kissed her softly, making her toes curl. He pulled away just enough to mumble against her lips. “Then it’s settled. Tomorrow, we’ll have breakfast and tour all of Castle Belmont’s grounds. It’s your home now too.”

“And what about today?” she asked breathlessly.

“Today, you’re mine.” His lips pulled into a mischievous smirk.

Adelaide smiled. Leaning in to press her lips against his once more, she said, “And every day after too.”

Acknowledgements

I am not a big risk taker. As an introvert, I struggle to put myself out there or join in on group things. But when I saw the call for the *Tempting Thieves* collaboration at three a.m. one winter night, there wasn't anything to stop me from taking a leap of faith, and I'm so glad I did!

Thank you to Angela J. Ford and Stephanie BwaBwa for hosting such an amazing collaboration and inviting me to participate! I've loved being a part of this and getting to connect with other authors, many of whom whose books I admire too. This was such a crazy dream come true, and while *TSAF* sometimes tested my sense of who I am as an author, I'm beyond grateful for the opportunity and friendships built through this collaboration.

I'm thrilled to have had the opportunity to work with Ireen Chau and Saint Jupiter on the character illustrations and cover art! I can't thank y'all enough for bringing Adelaide and Gavin to life, and for the beautiful designs that brought the themes, elements, and symbols of *To Sway a Flame* to life.

There aren't enough words to express my gratitude to my fantastic editors, Ashley, Kate, and M.A.! Thank you so much for all of your help, your insights, and your friendship throughout my author journey, especially with *TSAF*. Whenever I start to get in my own head about my writing, I can count on y'all to help pull me out of it. I'm forever grateful and honored to work with you three! #HeirsSquadForever!

I wouldn't be where I am today without the support of my family. I'm sadly running out of ways to thank them, but I'm going to try anyway. THANK YOU all so much for your love, support, and sense of humor. I couldn't have done this without y'all. <3

Most of all, thank you to my readers! To those I've had the pleasure of meeting and to those who have picked my books up on a whim, THANK YOU SO MUCH! Getting to hear from you or chatting with you at signings brings me so much joy and is a big part of why I enjoy writing.

There are so many people who have supported me throughout the years that it's hard to properly thank them all. From the bottom of my heart, thank you, for whatever part you've played in my life, big or small.

Did you know that reader reviews are like gold to indie authors?

For authors, reviews not only give our books some social clout, but they also help readers just like you discover their next read!

Leaving the star rating of your choice and even a line or two about what you honestly thought of the book is a huge boost to indie authors and our book's long-term success. And who knows how many readers like yourself you'll be helping along the way by posting what you thought of the book on retail platforms, your social media, book sites like Goodreads, or on your own blog?

I would be forever grateful if you could leave a review and help me grow as an author.

Happy reading!

Brianna R. Shaffery

Let's Connect!

Don't forget to follow me on social media for insights into my life as a writer, fun behind-the-scenes tidbits, and the latest updates on my author journey!

Facebook: @BRSWritesOfficial
Instagram: @brs_writes
Tumblr: @world-of-fire-and-flight
TikTok: @brswrites

About the Tempting Thieves Collection

Tempting Thieves is a multi-author romantasy collection featuring cunning thieves who outsmart relentless hunters, steal forbidden treasures, and find love along the way. With enemies-to-lovers tension, slow-burn longing, forced proximity, secret identities, only one bed, and grumpy/sunshine dynamics, every story delivers an irresistible fantasy escape. Each book in the collection is a standalone. Read in any order.

Next in the Series: *To Sway a Trickster* by Jes Drew

She sacrificed everything for her people. He will do whatever it takes to save himself. Their marriage is the last hope for peace.